The Cit

Book Two of the Chronicles of the

Second Interstellar Empire of

Mankind

By

Robert I. Katz

The City of Ashes:

Book Two of the Chronicles of the Second

Interstellar Empire of Mankind

Cover design by Steven A. Katz

Also by Robert I. Katz

Chapter 1

Two weeks after the siege of Aphelion finally ended, we set out for Gath. It was a boring two weeks. The streets were cleaned, the power grid fixed and reinforced. The city's infrastructure was inspected, repaired and made sound. Our allies' troops were wined and dined and given the keys to the city, which they richly deserved. As for myself, I had little to do except tend to my business interests and think about the future. I was eager to get started.

Guild Master Anderson had meant it when he said that we would be putting on a show. We travelled in one of the largest airships in the fleet, named the *Endeavor*, re-painted for our trip in all the colors of the Meridien flag, festooned with rippling pennants and banners flapping in the breeze. The personnel, however, were intended to put on a very different sort of show, all either elite military or secret service, about a third female. All of them moved with quiet confidence. All of them looked like they could punch through walls and probably most of them could.

"Bring somebody with you," the Guild Master had said. "Gath is a chauvinist culture. They will expect a young, virile man like yourself to have a sexual outlet."

"Why should we care what they expect?" I said, though I had no objection in principle to a sexual outlet.

"Think of it as an insurance card. If you bring a woman along, it will make it harder for their spies to seduce you." He shrugged. "No doubt, they'll still try, but why make it easy for them? If you don't have anybody in mind, we'll assign a member of the military." He got a far-away look on his face. "That might be best, actually, a combination mistress and bodyguard."

I looked at him, not quite scandalized. "That seems above and beyond the call of duty."

"We wouldn't insist that she have sex with you. She could pretend."

I declined his offer of military assistance for my libido but did ask Jennifer to come along, though I felt it wiser to not mention the Guild Master's comments regarding our hosts' expectations in the bedroom. "Sounds interesting," she said. "Sure." She grinned. "I'm looking forward to it."

So, we drifted over Imperion, Cuomo, Valspur, Neece and the desert kingdom of Kush, which, like Gath, preferred to maintain the old ways. Kush rejected most modern technology outside of health care and genetically engineered crops. And air conditioning, pretty much a necessity when the average daily temperature during most of the year hovers over forty degrees Celsius. The Kushians trailed below our ship on horseback, carrying long rifles to protect themselves against sand-tigers and the lizard-like morions, drawing pictures with wax stylets on sheaves of paper and talking among themselves. They had one unusual but obviously useful modification: like chameleons, they could change color to blend into their surroundings, which varied from tan sandstone to red, iron rich rock. They seemed interested in our passage and thankfully didn't try to shoot us down. I wondered if they had holo connections and were fans of the upcoming games.

We took our time. We wanted to be seen. The ship stopped twice, both times to pick up passengers. Denali was a small mountainous nation in the center of the continent, lumber, harvested from enormous hardwood trees, being their principal product. McClain was the only city, neatly laid out in a grid around the government center. The *Endeavor* floated to a mooring atop the Parliament building. We exited the ship, met the Prime Minister and his cabinet, had lunch at a restaurant that specialized in wild game, and trooped back into the ship before nightfall.

John Mead was the passenger, a big man with a perpetual smile, he moved slowly, as if careful not to damage other, more delicate human beings. I knew of John Mead. He had trained at the same dojo as Master Chen and owned a chain of martial arts academies that spread across the continent.

Denali, like so many nations in the wake of Gath's challenge, had suddenly awakened to their own danger. Alliances were being made. Denali had entered into negotiations with the Guild Council and it had been decided that I would not be alone in entering the Grand Tournament.

Fine with me, not that I had anything to say about it.

John Mead looked at me with mild interest when we first met, as if wondering what made me think that I might have a chance at winning against the best fighters in Gath. I smiled back and let him wonder. At least, he was polite.

The mountains turned into foothills, then a high plain and a day later, we came to Hayden, a town on the edges of Lake Sierra, the third largest body of fresh water on the continent. Hayden was the home town of Alessandro Abruzzi. I had heard of him, as well. Five years before, he had entered the Grand Tournament of Gath, the only foreigner that year, and he had done better than anybody had expected, ranking forty-fifth out of the nearly five thousand who had entered. Apparently, he had decided to try again, and we were elected to help him do it.

Alessandro Abruzzi was not quite so pleasant as John Mead. Along with the Captain, a hard-eyed navy man named Reece Jones, his first mate, Commander Boyd and John Mead, I was part of the greeting party as Abruzzi entered the ship. Abruzzi gave Mead a little bow, which Mead returned. He glared at me, his lips wrinkling. We shook hands and he squeezed. I smiled and squeezed back. Abruzzi's hand was not quite as hard as granite and just a bit smaller than a boulder but his hand was no stronger than mine. After a moment, he loosened his fingers. I was tempted not to loosen mine, but we weren't there to make enemies. I let go. He clenched and unclenched his fist, the knuckles audibly cracking, nodded abruptly, turned to the Captain and was perfectly polite for the rest of the evening.

Both Abruzzi and Mead traveled alone. Apparently, neither of them were worried at the prospect of being seduced by the sinister agents of Gath, but then, perhaps neither of them were spies.

As the putative guests of honor, Jennifer and I ate at the Captain's table every night, along with the other officers, and now, John Mead and Allesandro Abruzzi. Like Abruzzi, I don't think most of the crew took me seriously, not at first. One junior lieutenant named Jeffrey Grant seemed particularly contemptuous. He looked at Jennifer at my side, grimaced, turned to an ensign and made a little comment about delusional rich men and their mistresses. I don't think that he intended me to hear him but he obviously didn't care much if I did.

7

I pondered his smug, smiling face for a long moment. I hadn't kept my abilities secret, not deliberately, but it had been a long time since I had fought competitively and back then, it had been entirely within the confines of the Guild Hall, and Guild members don't talk to outsiders about what happens within the Guilds. In the Guild, and in the world of business and industry, I was a respected player, but this was a different world.

There are two approaches to dealing with an opponent, any opponent: you can try to take them by surprise or you can try to intimidate. I didn't like Allesandro Abruzzi's attitude. John Mead was more polite about it but somehow, I suspected that he shared Abruzzi's opinion. I resented that opinion, and I didn't like Junior Lieutenant Jeffrey Grant. Maybe it was time to show what I could do...we were supposed to be putting on a show, after all.

"Captain?" I said.

"Yes, Mr. Oliver?"

"Would you mind very much if I demonstrated to Mr. Grant the error of his ways?"

The Captain eyed Lieutenant Grant and smiled slowly. "Certainly not," he said. "It would be educational for him and entertaining for the rest of us."

"Excellent." I raised my voice. "Lieutenant Grant," I said. "I could use some exercise." I smiled. "Perhaps you would like to spar with me later this evening?"

A sudden silence fell over the table. I doubt that the rest of the officers were exactly on my side but none of them thought much of Grant. He found himself the sudden center of attention and obviously didn't like it. His face turned red and he quickly swallowed the food in his mouth. "I'd love to," he said.

"Good."

I noted that John Mead kept his face impassive during this exchange. Abruzzi gave me a doubtful look, then shrugged his massive shoulders.

The rest of the meal was subdued. Jennifer and I wandered back to our suite after dinner. "You sure about this?" she asked.

"Oh, yeah," I said. "After the last few weeks? I'm in no mood to put up with any more bullshit."

She smiled. "Okay," she said. That was just one of the things that I liked about Jennifer. She knew when to push and when to leave it alone and she always knew the score.

An hour later, we walked into the gym to find it packed. Bleachers rose up along the walls, filled with what seemed to be the entire ship's personnel. A nine-meter octagonal shaped ring stood in the center. This surprised me a little, as the military generally preferred the smaller Sumo type circle for practice and training bouts, but then Gath used the octagon and Gath was where we were going, so it made sense.

Grant wore a black gi. I came in wearing a white robe and when I stripped it off the room fell silent for a moment, before the buzz of excited conversation came back a little louder. Under the robe, I had on only black trunks and black canvas shoes with rubber soles. Neither the shoes nor the trunks were new and my legs and torso were roped with muscle. I looked like I knew what I was doing, which I did. I smiled at Grant and he frowned, looking for the first time uncertain. We walked to the center of the cage. The referee gave his instructions, dropped his arm and I whirled, sweeping Grant's legs out from beneath him. He fell heavily, jumped to his feet and glared. I smiled back at him.

"Point," the referee said.

We walked again to the center of the ring and stood facing each other until the referee gave the signal. This time, I waited for Grant to demonstrate what he could do. He came in fast and threw a series of punches at my face. I shook them off with quick flicks of my wrists, stepped in and hit him with an uppercut to the abdomen. Hard. He dropped, wheezing.

"Point," the referee said.

I shook my head. Grant wasn't bad, exactly. Actually, he was pretty good. He had to be, to be a part of this crew. He just wasn't nearly as good as he thought he was. Any pro would have torn him apart.

Now, he was seriously pissed off. He snarled at me while the referee raised his arm and dropped it, and then he charged. I jumped, grabbed his torso between my open legs, twisted and let the momentum carry us to the mat. I slithered around his back, levered his wrist across my chest and hyperextended his elbow. An armbar.

9

If I wanted to, from this position, I could snap his joint. The crowd grew silent. Grant groaned but didn't tap out. I put a little pressure on the joint, which hurts. It hurts a lot. "Fuck!" he yelled and slapped the mat with his opposite hand. I let him go and jumped to my feet. Grant took a few seconds longer to get up. His face was white and he rubbed his arm. I didn't trust Grant. His aura flared, almost crackling. We were both supposed to exit at the same time from opposite sides of the ring but I could see him hesitate. "Don't," I whispered. "You'll regret it." He looked me in the eyes, his lips thin, his breath coming fast and then I could see him deflate. He put his head down, turned and walked out.

Most of the crowd looked happy. A few seemed disappointed. John Mead gave me a speculative look. Allesandro Abruzzi frowned. The Captain said something that I couldn't hear to Commander Boyd and chuckled. I could see money changing hands but on the whole, I could detect no animosity among the assembled audience. This was good. None of us knew what we would be getting into once we reached Gath but the crew was at least tentatively on my side. I was pleased. It was a good night's work.

Chapter 2

The City of Gath in the province of Gath in the nation of Gath was clean and orderly but it was nevertheless a drab and dreary place. The buildings were gray concrete, almost all of them large, squat and brooding. The populace also wore a lot of gray, highlighted by small epaulets and insignia in red, green, blue and purple. "It's a military dictatorship with communist overtones," Captain Jones said, "and it embodies the worst of both systems. There's a hereditary aristocracy and everybody else scrounges for the dregs."

"There are plenty of dregs," I said. "These people aren't starving."

"Oh, it's not a poor nation, but if they decided to drop the collectivist bullshit and encourage private industry, they might grow an actual, functioning economy. As it is, most of their capital goes to the military and the ruling class, which is pretty much the same thing. The land is fertile. Their farms are well run." The Captain wasn't telling me anything that I didn't already know. I shrugged. From my point of view, the relative weakness of Gath's social system was an advantage that I hoped to exploit.

We had reached the outskirts of the city a few hours before, opened concealed portholes on the top of the ship—where they couldn't be seen by ground based surveillance—and released a swarm of micro-recorders. The recorders drifted away from the ship like a smoky cloud. They were programmed to seek out government buildings, military installations and places with high population density. The recorders were inert until triggered, when they would release their data up into cyberspace. They were also explosive, just in case we needed a distraction. Finally, our ship drifted to a mooring on a spire at the top of a fifty-story tourist hotel. I had halfway expected to be subtly (or not so subtly) mistreated: room too small or too crowded or too cold, no hot water, lousy food. Nope. They wanted to demonstrate that their society was superior to all the others so foreigners, no matter their business, were treated royally, much better than the majority of their own citizens.

We left a skeleton crew up on the ship, which rotated daily, and the rest of us were housed in luxury, one whole floor of the hotel, deep, soft carpets, picture windows, superb food and drink, our own swimming pool and gym. Basically, everything anybody could wish for, including an offer of "comfort women" for the men and "comfort boys" for the females in the crew, or vice-versa, depending on preference. No doubt they were all spies and we wasted no time in turning down the offer, though a few lower ranking members seemed disappointed.

John Mead and Allesandro Abruzzi, not really members of our party, were given separate quarters of their own on a different floor. If they took advantage of the offer for companionship, I have no idea.

The games were due to start in two days, which meant two days to be bored and two days for our hosts to foment an incident. "They're not likely to pull anything right away," the Captain said. "Let the crew take leave but never in groups of less than five. Have them stay together."

Commander Boyd was a lean man with sharp eyes and a hooked nose. He looked older than his age but like all of the rest, was in excellent shape. He nodded, said, "Yes, sir," saluted and left to consult with the Sergeant-at-Arms.

The Captain sighed and shook his head. "Sooner or later, this is going to turn into a disaster. I can feel it."

"Probably," I agreed.

He made a rude noise, shook his head again and walked off.

My colleagues assumed that our rooms were bugged and since I could detect electromagnetic waves, I knew that they were. I could see the tiny whorls of energy at the base of a lamp, at strategic points in the walls, in the bed posts. "How do you feel about making love with an audience?" I asked Jennifer.

She grinned. "I'm all for it."

"Good," I said. "Me too."

We were encouraged to leave the hotel and partake of the myriad delights of Gath City. Official tours were offered but there was no requirement to take them. Wherever we went, we were surreptitiously followed by at least three Gathians in plain clothes,

12

soldiers, police or secret service, no way to tell. The crew was instructed to ignore them and they didn't bother us, just wandered along behind, not even pretending to mingle with the crowd.

The people of Gath appeared healthy and well fed. They were taller than average but few of them appeared happy. They walked along with a determined stride, unsmiling and rarely looking at their surroundings, but then there wasn't much worth looking at.

Jennifer and I went into a clothing store, just to see what they had. It was depressing. Little color, most of it variations on the standard gray civilian uniform, which looked much the same as the standard gray military uniform. Utilitarian, not ugly, exactly, but exceedingly drab. Jennifer felt the material of a few jackets and a skirt, frowning, then shrugged. "The cloth isn't flimsy. It's well made," she said. "Nobody would want to wear it back home, though."

"I don't know. You might start a trend."

She wrinkled her nose. "I doubt it."

We stopped at a restaurant for lunch and were given a table by the window. Our unofficial escort sat down at a table nearby. They did nothing obvious but the crowd seemed to recognize them for what they were and we were given a wide berth. There wasn't a lot of choice on the menu: a chicken breast, a pork cutlet and a small piece of steak, with grilled vegetables on the side. The food was hearty but bland and under-seasoned. A little salt and pepper improved it, though, and we almost enjoyed it. The other diners gave us curious looks but otherwise appeared to ignore us.

A hologram played in a corner near the ceiling, a military parade. The voice was turned down too low for us to make out the words but the presenter seemed to be extolling the wondrous virtues of the fatherland. Another holo in the opposite corner ran a feature on the upcoming games. There wasn't much conversation in the restaurant and I don't think it was because of us. These people were not in the habit of revealing their thoughts in public. I wondered if it was any different when they were in private. Probably not. Such regimes tended to have a lot of spies and even your kids might wind up turning you in if you said too much of the wrong thing.

We wandered through a public park, which did have a few shrubs and scraggly trees but was mostly covered in exercise equipment, which groups of young people were diligently using. After another hour of wandering around and finding little worth seeing, we gave up and returned to the hotel.

Chapter 3

The stated purpose of the Grand Tournament was to identify potential military assets among the populace: the best fighters, the best strategists, potential leaders. The fact that every five years, the Grand Tournament also rubbed the world's collective face in the facts of Gath's superiority was an unstated—but to the government of Gath—an equally valid and important purpose. Prizes were given at all levels of the competition and for the average citizen of Gath, success in the Grand Tournament was the surest, quickest way to promotion.

"Check," I said.

My opponent frowned down at the board and then gave me an angry look. I didn't feel sorry for him. You take nothing for granted in chess. It doesn't matter what an opponent looks like; he could be a beginner at the game or he could be a grandmaster. A skinny little guy with buck teeth and glasses is just as likely to have the soul of an assassin. So, you play every game as if it counts and treat every opponent with respect, if not fear.

This guy, however, wasn't very good. It was an elimination tournament and we were both playing our second match, which meant that both of us had already won or at least drawn our first game, but he must have gotten lucky or maybe his opponent was just lousy.

I was not a grandmaster but I was pretty good at the game. I had gained a one pawn advantage early on and then traded pieces. One of the principles of endgame strategy is to simplify both positions as quickly as possible. Once you have an advantage, you want to reduce the available options. I had done so. My opponent stared at the board for a long time but staring was not going to change his position. Finally, he sighed, glared at me, shook his head and tipped over his king. I glanced at my interface. I had an hour for lunch before the next bout.

My next opponent was better. He had white and opened with a King's gambit, which frankly, rarely works. White trades a pawn for a supposedly superior position but in the end, the trade is hardly ever worth it. We exchanged pieces for almost thirty moves and the game ended in a draw. I was satisfied with a draw. A draw wouldn't hurt me.

My last opponent of the day was a highly rated player but he made a classic mistake: he fell for his own propaganda. He didn't know me but he knew I was a foreigner and he knew that foreigners are inherently inferior to the glorious natives of Gath. It was probably unconscious on his part but he just assumed that I didn't know what I was doing. He started out sloppy, lost a pawn early on and by the time he realized that he was in trouble, it was too late. He lost a game that he should have won.

"How did it go?" Jennifer asked.

"So far, so good. Better than expected, anyway. I won three and drew one."

We were sitting in the hot tub, sipping wine. "That's good." Jennifer put her glass down, leaned over and kissed me. "Have you ever had sex in a hot tub before?" she asked.

"Once or twice," I said.

She grinned. "You can't have too much sex in a hot tub." She kissed me again and moved on top.

Yep. So far, so good.

I lost the next morning to a guy with a grandmaster rating, which knocked me out of the chess portion of the tournament but I had accumulated a lot of points. They wanted to winnow the field, and we were already down to fewer than a thousand contestants. John Mead and Allesandro Abruzzi, I was interested to see, were still in it.

The three of us had exchanged very few words during our voyage. Mead and Abruzzi had deliberately avoided each other, and myself as well, except for dinner at the Captain's table, where neither of them had said more than a few words. One day, however, I came upon Mead in the ship's library, a carpeted room with sturdy wooden book cases. The books were carved wooden shells containing electronic readers, each stuffed with many thousands of copies on every subject imaginable.

The room was entirely whimsical, since any of us could call up any volume we wished on our own personal interface, it's real purpose to allow private meetings in a comfortable, soothing atmosphere. I wasn't looking for Mead and I wasn't interested in looking for a book. I was restless, exploring the ship, merely out of curiosity, and here he was, sitting in an easy chair, looking at a volume on Renaissance art.

I nodded when I saw him sitting there, and began to close the door.

"Please," he said, "come in."

I hesitated and Mead smiled at me. It was the most expression I had yet seen on his face. I stepped in and closed the door.

"I was hoping for an opportunity to speak with you," he said.

I sat down in a soft leather chair. "Why is that?"

"Stephen approves of you. That intrigued me."

"Stephen?"

"Stephen Sarnoff." Seeing my bewilderment, he grinned and said, "Master Chen."

"Ah…" It occurred to me belatedly that I had never before heard my sensei's real name.

"We trained together, way back when, in the same dojo. He liked to play practical jokes."

"He did?" Somehow, I couldn't see the grave, controlled sensei as a player of jokes.

"I keep in touch with him. I spoke with him shortly after the invasion of your capital city. He told me that you planned on entering the tournament in Gath."

I pondered that. I hadn't told Master Chen my plans beyond what had been publicly announced but it wouldn't be difficult to figure out what we were doing. It was obvious, after all. We wanted it to be obvious.

Mead gave me a searching look. "He says that you are skilled, a diligent pupil. I wanted you to know that I bear you no ill will but I am going to do my best in the upcoming tournament."

"Of course," I said. "I would expect no less. This isn't personal. So will I."

He shrugged. "It might not be personal to you or to me but it is very personal to many others."

"Abruzzi," I said.

"I know Allesandro Abruzzi only by reputation. He is a talented fighter but he allows his emotions to get in his way. Be careful around him."

"Thank you," I said. "I will."

I had also spoken just once with Abruzzi. The day following my little demonstration with Lieutenant Grant, Abruzzi made a point of coming up to me in the gym. We were both dressed in work-out clothes. Abruzzi's body looked like it was carved out of rocks. He watched me on the bench press for a moment, waited until I had put the weights back in their rack, then said, "You're not quite the pretty boy that you appear. I wanted you to know that I know that."

Okay. Good that we got that off our chest. "And now that you know it, so what?"

He gave me a brooding look. "It doesn't matter what you look like," he said. "It doesn't matter that you think you know how to fight. If you get in my way, I will go through you."

Yes, yes, yes...blah, blah, blah. You are without doubt the greatest fighter in the Universe, and your terrified opponents will look upon your magnificence and despair. "I'll keep it in mind," I said.

He glared, turned and walked away.

After the chess tournament, I rotated onto a virtual reality simulation. It was a standard scenario, with lots of dark forests, rushing rivers and drizzling rain. I was a private in the king's army. My platoon had been sent on a scouting mission and stumbled on a horde of invading goblins. Now, we were trapped, surrounded on three sides. Our only chance of breaking out was to swim a raging river back to our own army's position on the other side of the water.

Piece of cake.

I took it upon myself to cover the retreat, bobbing and ducking, swinging my sword, cutting off goblin heads and arms and legs and having a merry old time until all my comrades were in the river and then I jumped in and began to swim along with them toward the farther shore...until an arrow hit me in the back. A buzzer sounded. I was officially dead and out of the scenario but I had demonstrated both skill and initiative. Privates, like pawns, are expendable.

Privates are expected to die but the way I died counted for a lot. At this level of the game, I couldn't have done any better.

The next level up was Sergeant. I organized the retreat, gathered the men together, wasted a few privates in the process and got most of us out alive. Again, I racked up points to the max. By the time the game ended, late in the day, I was fifth in the overall standings, out of more than eight hundred competitors left in the contest.

John Mead was seventh. Allesandro Abruzzi was seventeenth.

The next day was simple: running and lifting. I came in fiftieth in the lifting portion of the competition. Since there were no weight divisions, I was competing against men (and a few women) who outweighed me by a considerable margin and I was pleased with my score.

The races were divided into sprints and distance. I came in fifth in the hundred meters and fourth in the ten thousand. All in all, a pretty good day's work. My overall score drifted up from fifth to fourth.

The obstacle course came next. I wasn't looking forward to this. In the past, a lot of competitors had crashed out on the obstacle course. We ran one by one, another contestant crossing the starting line every minute. We had been given a map and so we all knew what to expect in general terms but we would have to discover the details for ourselves.

The course was five kilometers long. I ran across a flat track for a hundred meters, and then jumped a fence. Two others of increasing height quickly followed. I had to climb the last one, which slowed me down for a few seconds and then I came to a rock wall. We had been given knives but neither ropes nor pitons. The sheer granite face had minute indentations for hands and feet but if we fell, it was going to hurt, or worse. Enhanced strength gave me a slight advantage but most of the competitors, the ones who were left, at least, were both strong and fast. No matter.

The sun was hot, the sky a cloudless blue. Thankfully, there was no wind. I dug my fingers into small holes in the rock, went up as fast as I could and didn't look down. A few minutes later, I got to the top and ducked as a swinging wooden pole swept over my head. I waited two seconds, hauled myself up, jumped over the pole on its next pass and ran down a grassy, muddy trail. The trail looked...odd. Bare patches were spaced at suspiciously even intervals. I stopped for an instant, picked up a large rock and dropped it onto one of the bare patches. It fell in. I peered into the hole; at least half a meter deep. If I had fallen into one of these, I could easily have broken a leg, and of course, the grassy parts of the trail could contain traps, as well. I ripped a branch from one of the trees, stripped the leaves and used it as a staff, probing the ground in front of me as I walked. All the bare patches covered holes and one grassy area, near the end of the trail, covered another.

Clever, I thought. The bastards.

I ran on. The trail ended in what appeared to be a thick copse of nearly impenetrable forest. I had to drop my improvised staff but I grabbed an overhead branch, swung myself up into the trees and kept going, jumping from tree to tree like a squirrel. Vines hung at convenient intervals but somehow, it didn't seem smart to try swinging on them. I stopped for a moment, however, and used my knife to cut a nice length of vine, wrapped it around my waist and tied it. It might come in handy later. Nothing untoward occurred in this part of the course and a few minutes later, the forest ended at the edge of a rushing stream.

According to the map, the stream was less than half a meter deep but it looked a lot deeper, the water dark and tumbling over submerged rocks. Well, if it worked once, it ought to work again. I used the knife to cut a tree branch and made another staff, then probed the streambed with the staff and as I suspected, the water plunged into a hole almost two meters deep. I unwrapped the vine from around my waist, tied it around a rock and threw the rock between two closely spaced boulders on the opposite side. I pulled back until the rock caught between the boulders then I waded out into the water. I almost lost my balance but held onto the vine, pulling myself through the water hand over hand. The current helped. It dragged me downstream and the vine swung me around and close to the opposite bank.

I got my legs under me, regained my footing and went on over a paved pathway until I reached a flat rubberized surface that stretched for two kilometers straight to the end of the course. The track was designed to let those who still had the energy push themselves through and maybe even gain a few seconds. I ran.

A few minutes later I could see the finish line. Only one obstacle left: a maze full of swinging, weighted poles suspended from a frame overhanging the last hundred meters. The poles were set to come down at random times and variable speeds. No help for it. I entered the maze, stopped as one pole passed in front of my face, jumped over another, barely dodged a third. There was no way to do this fast. If I tried, I would get slaughtered. I stopped, started, stopped, started, gaining a few centimeters, maybe sometimes a meter or more, worked my way to the end as quickly as I could and crossed the line.

Dimly, I could hear the crowd. Some were cheering but the cheering was muted. I glanced at the scoreboard. My time in the obstacle course was the third best, which put me into third place in the overall standings. I was the only foreigner left in the main competition and the good residents of Gath were not exactly pleased.

I drew a deep breath. The sun was a red-golden ball on the horizon and I was finally done for the day.

Thank God. I needed a bath and a good night's sleep.

Chapter 4

My first actual fight took place the next day. It was almost a joke. My opponent was a skinny kid who had probably entered the competition on a dare. He had done well at chess, however, and moderately well against the goblins, so he was still in the overall tournament.

The number one rule of competition in the octagon is the same as it is for any other game: never underestimate your opponent, but in this case, it was hard. The kid was pale and almost trembling. He looked like he didn't want to be there and he probably didn't. The referee held up his hand, let it drop and for a moment, neither of us moved. The kid seemed confused. He turned his head from side to side, desperately looking for help but this was the last place anybody was going to help him. Finally, I glided forward into the fifty-four steps of the Goju Shiho. He stared at me. "Come on, kid," I said. "Do something." He cleared his throat and just stood there.

Okay. I moved into the Taikyoku Shodan, a kata which emphasizes low blocks and middle lunges, gliding closer and closer. I was two feet away from him when he gave an ear-splitting shriek, flipped forward and aimed a kick at my abdomen. Suddenly, he was smiling.

I suppose he thought that his pretense of bewildered incompetence had lulled me into underestimating him but I glided to the side and underneath his kick, grabbed him by the pants and flipped him upside down. He was fast, very fast actually and despite his little act, he must have thought he was hot stuff, but once you're in the air, you're committed. You can't change direction when your feet are off the ground but an opponent can change it for you. He came down hard on his head, flopped over on his back and was out cold.

What a jerk.

I bowed to the audience and the referee and walked out of the circle. I had a three- hour break before my next bout and I went back to the suite for a shower and some lunch. I knew that the majority of the *Endeavor*'s crew would be gathered in the media room, which had a wet bar, snacks, a fully equipped kitchen, padded chairs and couches and an enormous holo-screen in the center. A running commentary of the games kept the score constantly updated, so I decided to grab some food while watching the rest of the competition. Captain Jones looked up when I walked in. He frowned when he saw me. "Look at this," he said.

Two women were fighting with knives. The blades were dull but they had the weight and feel of the real thing and could do some damage if the fighter really tried. They were filled with red ink containing a nerve poison that would temporarily cause paralysis on the part of the body that was hit. One combatant had two red streaks on one arm, which was hanging limply at her side.

I stared. "Oh, shit," I said.

Captain Jones puffed up his cheeks and squinted at the screen. The two women closed with a flurry of action, almost too fast to make out any details but the woman with the red streaks was suddenly down on the mat and the other woman was sitting on her chest, holding her blade across her opponent's neck.

"Bout," the referee called.

The winner jumped to her feet and bounced twice, both arms raised over her head. Then she turned to the camera and gave a dazzling, deranged smile.

It was Jennifer.

"Why should you have all the fun?" Jennifer asked.

I sighed and decided to keep my mouth shut. I dug my fingers into her flesh, kneading her back. She groaned. "Just like that," she said. "You give an excellent massage."

I knew that Jennifer was good. Just like me, if she had wanted to fight professionally, she could have gone far. We had sparred occasionally and I had to really work to keep ahead of her. She was fast, accurate and ruthless when she wanted to be but somehow, I had expected her to stay in the background, keep a low profile and play her appointed role as my devoted, dutiful mistress. Stupid of me.

It wasn't like there were no other foreigners in the games. There were a lot of them, but in prior years, none aside from Allesandro Abruzzi had ever gone beyond the third level of the competition. I was counting on doing much better than that. I was planning on rubbing Gath's nose into the fact that they were a bunch of provincial idiots with delusions of grandeur. Jennifer's participation was just another thing to worry about. I suppose I must have sighed again.

"Relax," she said. "I can take care of myself."

Maybe she could, maybe she couldn't but in the end, Jennifer was a free agent and there wasn't a thing that I could do to stop her.

"Be careful," I said.

"I haven't entered the main competition, just the knife tourney. I like knives." She turned her head to the side and gave me a knowing smile. "Anyway, I'll be just as careful as you," she said.

Yeah. That's what worried me.

Combat was a round robin, not a direct elimination, not exactly, but each bout was scored on a system that gave points for strength, speed and demonstrated skill. Injuries were quickly treated. We wore padded shoes, gloves and headgear, since they didn't want the contestants to be so damaged that they could not continue, but after the first day, those on the bottom were informed that they would not be allowed to continue.

There were two bouts each on the first day, only one the next, and as the weaker contestants were eliminated from the competition, we were given a recovery day between each bout.

I had three more bouts over the next few days, winning them all, and my points were tallied. Jennifer also had three more. She won two but lost her final bout to a brunette Amazon who moved like lightning and outweighed her by twenty kilograms. Still, she did very well and she was a favorite with the crowd. I was just glad that we both got through the rest of the week without injury.

John Mead had blown through his competition, wining each bout with economy and flair, but his next opponent was a very large, very fast guy from the Navy of Gath, named Errol Aziz. According to the official playbook, Aziz had won the personal combat division of the Grand Tournament five years before but hadn't finished in the top one hundred overall. Apparently, strategy and tactics was not his thing. This year, he hadn't bothered to enter the Grand Tournament, only personal combat.

The unofficial information floating around the web was more worrisome. Errol Aziz hadn't lost a bout in more than seven years, and his opponents had a tendency to suffer injuries.

They went back and forth for three rounds, neither giving an inch and neither getting in more than a glancing blow. This guy was very, very good and Mead...he was a revelation. He flowed like liquid around the ring, twisting, contorting, always in perfect balance, light and swift and sure. Neither one seemed to tire. Neither gave an inch...and then, somehow, unaccountably, Mead missed what should have been a routine roundhouse kick and Errol Aziz shattered his knee cap.

This was an off day for me. I was sitting in a booth near the ring but despite the fact that I was watching closely, I couldn't see exactly what happened. Mead wasn't just good, he was fantastic. There was no way he should have missed the way he did...except that he did.

Medical care in Gath was excellent. When I dropped in on Mead a couple of hours later, he was lying in bed, his leg in a regeneration cast, looking glum. He seemed taken aback when I walked into the room. "I wasn't expecting to see you," he said.

Mead and I were hardly close. Still, I admired the man. He fought fairly and treated his opponents with respect. I shrugged. "How are you doing?"

His lip quirked upward. "Could be worse," he said.

"I was watching. I couldn't see what happened."

Mead sighed. "*Life is short but art is long*. Hippocrates. What we do is an art. It isn't real. It's an art designed to simulate mortal combat but it is not, in fact, mortal combat. The art has form. It has structure, and it has rules." He shook his head. "There are no rules in war. We should never forget that."

I stared at him. "What are you saying?"

He gave me a quick, half-hearted grin. "One of the moves that I've become known for, perhaps a little too well known, is to use the ropes as a springboard. It's a useful way to gain a little extra height on my kicks. I don't do it often, perhaps once every other bout. The rope was looser than it should have been."

"They cheated?"

He shrugged. "I can say with certainty that the rope was looser than it should have been. I have no way to tell if anybody cheated. They may have. I, however, will recover and for that, I'm grateful...but I'm out of the tournament."

The ever-present bugs were twinkling in my sight, ten of them scattered around the room. Mead's escort of Gathian troops as well as my own, clustered in the hallway outside the room. "Nothing we can do about it," I said.

"No." He looked at me and gave a regretful smile. "Take care. I suspect that you'll need it."

Two hours later, I was watching as Allessandro Abruzzi fought a Lieutenant in the army of Gath named Omar Rasim. Rasim was young. This was his first tournament. He had a good record in his bouts so far but he was outclassed from the very beginning. Abruzzi didn't have the same lithe style as John Mead. With his body habitus, there was no way he could. Abruzzi was a strong. He was built to crush. He was still fast, though. His kicks and punches came out of nowhere. He stalked his opponent across the ring, cutting off the angles until Rasim had nowhere left to go. Once Abruzzi got his hands on him, it was quickly over. Abruzzi slid up Rasim's body and got him in a chokehold and Rasim tapped out before Abruzzi broke his neck.

Abruzzi didn't showboat. He rose to his feet, bowed to his opponent and the crowd and matter-of-factly left the ring.

Rasim had been good but in the end, he was overmatched. I wondered how Abruzzi would do against one of the top fighters. I found out soon.

The last bout of the next day was one the crowd was eagerly looking forward to: Allessandro Abruzzi against Errol Aziz. They entered the ring at the same time, listened stolidly as the referee gave instructions and bowed, first to the referee, then to each other. The bell rang.

Neither one of them attacked immediately. Aziz turned to the side. Abruzzi turned with him. They began to circle, slowly spiraling in. Aziz snapped a kick. Abruzzi flowed away from it, reversed and aimed a kick of his own. Aziz moved his head and the kick swept by.

Both of them were big. Both were strong and fast and in perfect shape. Neither of them had lost a bout in many years. Looking at them together, the sure-footed confidence, the economy of their moves, with no wasted motion, I couldn't pick a winner.

Abruzzi feinted to the left. It was an excellent feint, barely perceptible, and it was enough to cause Aziz to shift his stance, just a little. Abruzzi came in from the right. Aziz met him, blocked, countered, blocked and then they were apart, still circling. Aziz had taken a hit to the mouth, not enough to draw blood, so fast I could barely see it. Abruzzi had a slight swelling under his left eye.

Aziz stepped in with a punch to the ribs. Abruzzi slipped it, aimed a punch of his own, which Aziz evaded. Abruzzi dropped, aimed a circle kick at Aziz' legs. Aziz did a reverse somersault and landed lightly on his feet.

The crowd loved it. Aziz was the obvious favorite and about a quarter of the crowd were roaring encouragement but most kept silent, intent on seeing every movement of the fight, and this included me. It was far more than appreciation for the sport. The draws had been published and I was acutely aware that sooner or later, if both of us lasted that far into the competition, I would be facing the winner of this match.

Gath took their fighting seriously. This wasn't the sort of bout I was used to, three points to the victor, a maximum duration of three rounds lasting three minutes each. This fight would go on, round after round, until one contestant gave up or could no longer continue. The referee's job was to keep some semblance of order but there were no judges and no ties.

The first round ended with a flurry of action but no damage that I could see. I might have given a slight edge to Abruzzi, since he seemed to have thrown a few more punches, but maybe not. The punches didn't seem to have had much effect. There were no style points and throwing more punches meant using more energy.

The second round began much like the first. A slow circle, shifting weight and stance, attention all on the opponent's center, a tentative feint and then a sudden, explosive burst of motion as they closed in, trading blows then spinning away. Both fighters kept at least one foot on the ground, which was smart. At this level of competition, a strike that could not be aborted made you vulnerable.

It was one thing to commit to a blow, quite another to find yourself with no way to counter.

Aziz spun and Abruzzi spun away but completed a turn and got a hand on Aziz' shoulder. He pushed but Aziz went with the throw, flipped over and wrapped both legs around Abruzzi's abdomen. Both of them fell to the matt and rolled, with Aziz on top. Abruzzi, far more limber than I would have given him credit for, contorted his opposite leg into a kick at Aziz' face, which landed, and Aziz let go. They both flipped back to their feet. I let out a breath I hadn't realized I was holding.

Maybe Aziz' attention lapsed, though that seemed hard for me to believe, or maybe Abruzzi saw an opening that I hadn't, but suddenly Abruzzi's left arm blurred and Aziz was spinning away and Abruzzi was on him, raining blows. Aziz tried to counter but he seemed dazed. He raised his arms, trying to ward off the blows and then the bell rang and the round was over. Abruzzi smiled at him and Aziz stood there for a moment, shaking his head and the both men went back to their corners, Abruzzi stalking across the ring, Aziz weakly shuffling.

Aziz seemed to recover by the start of the next round, though. Abruzzi tried to duplicate the punch that had staggered Aziz but Aziz merely shifted his head and the punch slipped by. There wasn't much action for the rest of the round. Both men seemed content to bide their time, recover their breath and study his opponent. The bell rang. They returned to their corners.

The next round was different. Perhaps Aziz felt that he now had something to prove. He came out in a blur of motion and launched into a roundhouse kick that nearly landed. An uppercut did and Abruzzi staggered back. A right cross barely missed. A left hook landed but Abruzzi was already moving with the punch and it didn't shake him. Abruzzi responded in kind with a spin and a kick to the abdomen that threw Aziz off balance, just for an instant, but Aziz shook his head and came in with a right cross that landed pretty squarely.

Blood was dripping from Abruzzi's nose. He ignored it. Aziz seemed to think that he had the advantage. He moved forward, throwing punches from all directions but Abruzzi spun into a circle kick and dropped, clipping Aziz below the knees. Aziz went down but Abruzzi was too far away from him to take advantage. Both men bounced back up and circled, throwing punches. Aziz landed a left hook. Abruzzi countered with an uppercut that might have ended the fight right then if it had connected squarely, and then the bell rang once again.

For a moment, both men stood there. Abruzzi's nose was still bleeding. Aziz' left eye was swelling. Both of them stalked back to their corners. The crowd roared. I could see money changing hands in the stands all around me.

And so it went for three more rounds, fast, vicious and bloody, but by the end of seven rounds I thought that maybe, just maybe, Abruzzi might have the advantage. Aziz seemed just a bit slower, his strikes the slightest bit weaker than they had been. Abruzzi seemed unshakeable, his nose still dripping blood, his left ear gouged, bruises on the right side of his face and his left torso, but just as fast as he was in the beginning.

The bell rang for the eighth and Aziz charged, jittering from side to side, feinting left, then right. He spun into a circle kick that barely missed, spun again and caught Abruzzi on the side of the face with a punch that didn't appear to have much force behind it but Abruzzi shook his head, then shook his head again and blinked. He appeared stunned.

Aziz gave him no chance to shake it off. In a flash, he flipped forward and swept Abruzzi's feet out from underneath. Abruzzi fell heavily to the mat and Aziz screamed and leaped and came down with both feet and all of his weight on Abruzzi's neck.

Necks are fragile. Tracheas are easily crushed. The referee cursed and pushed Aziz to the side and screamed for the medics, who rushed into the ring. Abruzzi's face was blue. His eyes bulged and his heels drummed against the ground. He convulsed, flecks of foam spewing from his lips.

They worked on him for twenty minutes while the crowd watched in growing silence but it was too late. Allessandro Abruzzi was dead.

Aziz stood in his corner, watching, his face impassive, his breath coming hoarsely, and finally, when Abruzzi's body was lifted onto a stretcher and taken away, the referee held up Errol Aziz' hand and declared him the winner of the match.

That night, we were all grim. I picked at my dinner. Jennifer stared at her plate. All of us ate in silence, the only sound the click of knives and forks against the plates and the clattering of the dishes. A few of the officers whispered to each other, glancing occasionally at me with worried eyes.

We had brought our own supplies, considering it foolish to trust any provisions that Gath might offer, though aside from the bugs, we had been treated with exquisite courtesy. The meal, as usual, was plentiful and well prepared but I barely tasted it. We had all known the risks but the tournament suddenly seemed much less like a game. Finally, the Captain gave a little shrug, turned to me and said, "Who are you fighting tomorrow?"

"Some kid. He's supposed to be good."

He glanced at the time. "Good luck, then." He rose to his feet, nodded to the rest and walked off without another word.

"Yeah," I said. "Thanks."

Chapter 5

I was in no mood to play around. The kid's name was Akmet Sen. He was twenty-three years old but carried himself like a professional. He fought well. He was fast and he was strong and he knew the moves. I thought about what Master Chen had said to me, all those years ago, about not relying too much on strength and speed. Master Chen had taught me well. You still had to know what you were doing. The kid did, but so did I, and I had been doing it a lot longer.

The bout lasted four rounds. He tagged me a couple of times. I felt my cheek swelling where he had connected with a jab but in the end, I flipped over, slithered around his back and got him in a rear choke hold. There was no way to break that hold unless he could get a hand on my wrist and was strong enough to pull my locked arms apart. He wasn't and he couldn't. He tapped out. We both rose to our feet and bowed. "Excellent bout," he said.

"Thanks," I said.

He grinned and his eyes drifted to the first row of spectators. "Errol Aziz is not happy."

I had of course seen Errol Aziz sitting there, intently watching the contest. "I hope not."

The kid nodded, his face thoughtful. "Still, he has never lost. I wish you luck but I won't be betting on you."

"Nothing I can do about that." Silently, I thought that I wouldn't bet on me, either.

He smiled. We bowed again and then we both exited the arena.

The freestyle tournament within the larger Grand Tournament was nearly over. My last bout would be with Errol Aziz. The tournament wasn't an elimination. The over all winner might be somebody other than Errol Aziz or myself, since many others had fought well. Still, unless I beat him, it probably would be Aziz. A few others had come close, most notably a giant named Celim Bakar, but nobody had won so decisively or in fewer rounds than Aziz.

I was not the only one who noticed that Errol Aziz had somehow wound up fighting the three most skilled foreigners, and that one of these three was now crippled and another dead.

Somebody was sending a message. The cheating, if it was cheating, might be suspected but it was not apparent, and without proof, who was going to protest? In any case, the nature of Aziz' victories was guaranteed to sow fear among his adversaries, and by extension to the adversaries of Gath. The battle will be different than you expect. You will never see the blow coming.

Okay. Errol Aziz was more than he appeared. So was I, and I could send messages as well.

Jennifer hugged me like she didn't want to let me go and I hugged her back. Finally, I said, "I gotta go."

"Yeah," she said. "I know." She kissed me, hard. "Come back."

"I'll do my best."

I watched her walk away, regretting for a long moment that I had ever agreed to this crazy scheme. Then I pulled myself together and turned to the Captain. "Let's do it," I said. An escort of Navy men in Meridien uniform accompanied me all the way into the arena and, not stepping away until we reached the steps of the octagon, speaking of sending a message. I arrived before Errol Aziz and leaned back against the ropes. None of them were loose.

Unlike John Mead, I had no signature moves. As a fighter, I was a relative unknown. Nobody here was quite sure what I could do in the arena but they knew by now that I was not to be taken lightly.

Aziz arrived a few moments later, along with the referee. I continued to lean against the ropes as he walked in, bounced a few times on his feet and raised his arms to the crowd. The crowd responded with a roar but it wasn't as loud a roar as it might have been. Aziz was their guy by default but he wasn't popular. They would rather see him win it than me, but they weren't about to go crazy for him.

Finally, he stopped bouncing, gave me a hard stare and stalked to the center of the ring. We both listened to the referee's pro forma instructions, and then the referee dropped his arm and Aziz charged straight ahead, his arms spread. I spun and my foot cracked against the side of Aziz' head but he was already moving in the direction of the kick. He went with the force, somersaulted to the side and rolled back to his feet. Then he smiled.

I hadn't hurt him. We both knew it but then, I hadn't expected to. He laughed softly, a low, throaty chuckle. He was letting me know that he could take whatever I could throw at him and still be standing there, undamaged.

I hoped he was bluffing.

I moved in, flicking punches at his head. His head jerked smoothly, hands in synch with mine, faster and faster until we stood in front of each other, trading blows. I got through his guard once and snapped his head to the side. He got through mine twice and my ribs ached but none of them seemed to be broken.

Kilo for kilo, I might have been stronger than him, but he had a lot more kilos. I might have been a touch faster. I might not. Maybe I had more stamina. Maybe I could last longer, tire him out and then pounce, but I had no reason to think so. He had lasted eight brutal rounds with Allessandro Abruzzi and I wasn't sure that I could do the same. It was going to come down to technique. Which of us was better trained in the art? Which of us could pull off a move that the other couldn't counter?

He might have been stronger but I was strong enough to knock him out if I could land the right punch. Not likely, though. He had the reach on me and his defense was excellent. Trading punches might be entertaining the crowd but wasn't doing either of us much good.

I dropped, swept my foot out and connected with his leading leg. He fell but rolled and bounced back up before I could take advantage. He tried to do the same thing to me but I jumped away before the sweep could connect.

The bell rang. We each returned to our corner and I tried to take stock. The crowd was happy. A lot of action but not much damage on either side. Aside from Master Chen (and I wasn't too sure even of Master Chen), I had never fought anybody better than Errol Aziz.

The bell rang. This time, Aziz was more cautious. We circled, neither attacking, not at first, both of us looking for that one moment, that one tiny opening when the other's defense might offer an opportunity. For almost a minute, we kept it up, circle, then pause, circle, pause.

I almost missed the attack when it came. One instant, he was standing, his attention focused on my center, the next, he was charging across the ring. I slid to the side, turned, elbowed him in the ribs, then turned, grabbed his wrist, dropped and pulled, kicking upward at his abdomen. It was a classic Tomoe-nage and it almost worked. He flew over me but instead of landing flat on his back, hopefully dazed, he managed to wrench his wrist from my grasp, went with the momentum, rolled forward, flipped off his hands and landed back on his feet, bouncing lightly. He grinned at me. "Good move," he said, then he charged, throwing punches.

I met him in the center of the ring but by now, I knew better than to stand there and let myself be battered. He was bigger, heavier, probably as fast and had a longer reach. He was far more likely to land a knock-out blow than I was. I twisted to the side, slid across his body and grabbed his wrist. I pulled him forward, slid to the mat with my right leg hooked around his left ankle and drove up and forward. Suddenly, he was down, with me on top.

My advantage lasted less than a second. He continued the roll and flipped me over. I went with it, landed on my feet and turned. He was already up, glaring.

The glare surprised me. It had been a routine enough move and he had countered it easily enough. And then I realized something…I was smaller than John Mead and Alessandro Abruzzi. I had no reputation as a fighter. Aziz had watched my bout with Akmet Sen but Sen hadn't been good enough to really push me.

I was better than he had expected. That surprised him. He had thought it would be easy. I smiled.

He gave a small nod of his head, smiled back and charged across the ring. I braced myself…but the bell suddenly rang. Aziz stopped, took a slow, deep breath and moved smoothly back to his corner.

A minute passed. The bell rang. Aziz moved out slowly, threw a few jabs, circling. I flicked away his punches, tried to move inside, then feinted left. He tried a snap kick that I evaded and he swept toward my head with an open palm. I moved my head back a centimeter and his hand went past. I smelled something, acrid and sharp. I blinked my eyes, then blinked them again…and my sight faded.

I was blind.

My hearing is almost as good as my sight. Bats and whales and dolphins, some birds, even tiny shrews have the ability to echo-locate and humans, even those without enhanced senses, have been known to learn the technique. I, however, had never bothered to learn it. I had never needed to.

Still, I could hear him, and my ability to sense auras depended on electrocytes under my skin, like those of an electric eel, not vision. He stood in front of me, gathering himself. I could hear the slither of his boots against the canvas. I could sense his aura against my skin. I could feel the soft rush of air as he moved forward. I did nothing. I stood there, blinking my useless eyes. I set aside my sudden desperation and I let him come. It was my only chance.

He wasn't subtle about it. His guard was no longer up. He no longer needed to guard himself, or so he thought. He threw a punch that started at his knees, his whole body behind it, aimed at my head. I could feel it. I could hear it. If that punch landed, it would be all over. I could hear the whoosh as his fist came flying at my face.

I moved my head back, just the smallest bit, and I stepped inside and he was there, just as I had known he would be. I wrapped both arms around his chest and drove forward. That, he was not expecting. He was startled and off-balance and we went crashing to the mat, with me on top. No time for niceties. No time for a second chance. I let the energy flow and a thousand watts of current snapped from my hands into his torso.

He screamed, his body spasming. It wouldn't last long. Once the current stopped, he would recover quickly and I had no way of knowing how long my blindness would last. Maybe forever. I had to end this and I had to end it now.

I slithered up his convulsing body, grabbed his head in both arms and twisted to the side. Errol Aziz shuddered once as his neck audibly snapped and then he lay still.

The crowd roared. I opened my mouth and I roared back as I staggered to my feet.

Fuck you, I thought. *Fuck you all.*

The ship's doctor examined me as soon as we returned to the hotel. There was nothing physically wrong with my eyes. The optic nerve was paralyzed. "It should wear off," he said, though he sounded uncertain, but indeed it did within a couple of hours. Jennifer fussed over me and I was happy to let her.

By the time I could see again, I wanted nothing more than a good dinner and a good night's sleep, except that I had trouble sleeping. I kept feeling Errol Aziz' vertebrae crunching under my fingers.

I kept wondering if I really had to kill him, but in the end, I knew that I had no choice. I was blind, and he had already killed Allesandro Abruzzi and at least temporarily crippled John Mead. I couldn't give him the chance to recover. I couldn't. It was possible, of course, that the referee would have declared him unfit to continue, but that was not likely. I knew my own capabilities. His muscles had been temporarily short-circuited but he wasn't truly unconscious. The electricity had been applied to his torso, not his head. No, if I hadn't killed him, he would have been back on his feet within seconds.

I would be glad when this was all over. I wanted to go home.

Chapter 6

The field had been winnowed. After the personal combat portion of the Grand Tournament, only twenty-five of us remained, twenty-three men and two women. We had an off day to recover, before the final challenge was to begin, and our generous hosts had something special in store for the evening. We were going to a party house, which served an important purpose in Gathian society. Similar to a private nightclub, with overtones of an ancient Geisha house, a bordello and an excellent restaurant and bar, such establishments were usually open only to government officials and military elite. They reminded me of Meridien's Guild houses but were considerably more exclusive in their clientele. And of course, none of the Guild houses had a bordello.

We were supposed to feel honored and somewhere, vaguely, I did, but mostly I just felt tired. No way to get out of it though, not without insulting our hosts.

"Watch out," Captain Jones said. "They'll probably try to seduce you or poison you. Maybe both."

Guild Master Anderson had said much the same thing. Glad to know we were all in agreement. Either or both did seem likely, and I really was not looking forward to this. Three Meridien soldiers were assigned to go along with me but there was only so much they could do if things turned ugly.

Jennifer, after all the points were tallied, had come in fourth in the knife tournament, more than respectable, but she hadn't been entered in the grand competition and was not invited to tonight's festivities. She didn't seem to mind. "I'll read a book," she said. "Have fun." Then she grinned. "A little fun. We wouldn't want you all tuckered out before tomorrow, now would we?"

And so, as night fell, my three guards and I walked through an arched gate into a small courtyard filled with stone walkways, flowers, a small, meandering stream and comfortable, carved stone benches. The walkway led to another arch, which opened into an enormous room filled with gaming tables, flashing lights, three raised stages and two trapeze artists flying back and forth overhead, with no net to catch them if they fell. None of the crowd seemed to pay them any attention.

On the wall above the door hung two framed pictures. The first was Atif Erdogan, the former head of the Presidium. He was large, middle-aged, a little stout, with a wide smile and bright shining eyes. He looked out of the portrait as if inviting the onlooker to participate in some great adventure. Next to him was a picture of Idris Kartal, the current head. Kartal was younger and thinner, with thick black hair, a trim black moustache and an intense look around the eyes. Kartal was not smiling. Kartal's look was a challenge, a demand, even. Join me, it seemed to say. Kartal did not look like a man given to compromise.

My guards were professionals. They surveyed the scene with dispassionate interest, gauging possible threats, but in reality, if our hosts decided to kill me, we could all be quickly overwhelmed. "Might as well get yourselves a drink," I said. "There's not much for you to do here."

The Sergeant in charge, Ben Franks, gave me a disapproving smile. "Not while we're on duty."

I shrugged. At that moment, a pleasant looking, middle-aged man, accompanied by four guards of his own, walked up to us. "Mr. Oliver," he said, and held out his hand for me to shake. "Gentlemen. I am Altan Deniz, the manager of Club Menagerie. You'll find your fellow competitors scattered throughout the room. All of us in our wonderful city have watched your exploits over the past few days with great admiration. No foreigner has ever risen so high in our competition. You are to be praised and congratulated." His smile thinned. "You might perhaps wish to know that the betting favorite is Celim Bakar, whose brother won the last grand tournament and is now a highly placed member of our ruling council."

I did know that. I had not yet encountered Celim Bakar but I had seen him fight. He was ten centimeters taller than me and twenty kilograms heavier and now that Errol Aziz was no longer with us, Celim Bakar's score in personal combat had been the highest, beating my total by a fraction. He had also beaten my score on the obstacle course and was currently leading the competition.

I also knew that the populace did not know what to make of my challenge. Newscasts were tightly controlled by the government.

Little mention had been made of the attacks on Meridien and none at all regarding any speculative involvement by Gath. The Grand Tournament, however, was open to the public and was televised all over the world. They had not been able to keep my successes a secret and so they had chosen to present me as a sort of exotic curiosity. Despite my current standing, nobody seemed to think that I might actually win.

I smiled at Altan Deniz and said, "I have a few tricks up my sleeve. Celim Bakar has no chance."

He blinked. His guards shuffled their feet. One of them frowned. "Well," Altan Deniz said, "we will wish you the very best of luck." He waved his hand at one of the stages, where an almost nude woman was singing a song with a lilting melody and a driving beat. "Please be aware that all costs and charges that you incur tonight are entirely to be borne by our government. Enjoy yourselves."

He nodded, smiled and walked away, to greet another customer.

"And fuck you, too," I muttered.

"They're not exactly into subtle here," Sergeant Franks said.

I shrugged. "Yeah. You can do what you want but I'm getting a drink."

The rank and file of Gath wore bland, gray uniforms, like a flock of dowdy pigeons. Their ruling class dressed like peacocks: gauze in all colors, sheer, see-through fabrics. They drank without restraint and danced with enthusiasm. In the darkened corners, I could see men caressing women and a few women slipping the clothes off their men. All three stages were occupied, one with a woman singer, one with a troupe of acrobats and one with a live sex show. I thought it curious that the acrobatic troupe had more spectators than the sex show.

The bar was crowded but I managed to squeeze my way up to the counter. The bartender, a tiny blonde dressed in a wisp of silk that allowed frequent glimpses of her rouged nipples, asked, "What will it be?"

"Whiskey," I said. "The best you've got."

She grinned, poured a generous shot into a crystal glass and set it in front of me. She didn't ask me for payment.

"Buy me a drink?"

I turned. Standing next to me was perhaps the most beautiful woman I had ever seen. Her hair was a rich chestnut and flowed in waves halfway down her back. Her face was shaped like a heart, with large eyes, full lips and a small, straight nose. Her body was spectacular. She wore a very short skirt and an almost transparent blouse.

"Sure," I said.

She grinned. "My name is Diamond."

She turned to the bartender and ordered a drink that I had never heard of. The bartender frowned but said nothing. She poured three different types of liquor into a shaker, added a few dashes of flavoring and a splash of soda and handed it to Diamond, who took a small sip and smiled. "I know who you are," she said. "I've been watching you on the holo."

A large man was suddenly standing next to Diamond. He glanced at me, his lips thinned and he said something in a foreign language to Diamond, which startled me. All nations on Illyria use Basic, a derivation of old Earth English. Few countries even have a language of their own. She didn't even look at him. She said something back in the same tongue and smiled into my eyes. The big man turned to me. "I am Celim Bakar," he said. "I know who you are. You should stay away from this one. She is trouble."

I studied him. His concern for me seemed real, which was entirely unexpected. "Thank you," I said. "I shall do my best to stay out of trouble."

He shook his head. "You have done well in the games. You are a worthy opponent." He glanced again at Diamond, who continued to ignore him.

Celim Bakar sighed. "Good luck," he said. He gave me a small, twisted smile. "I hope you survive the night."

"Thank you again." I looked at him. "I appreciate the advice."

He shook his head and walked off without another word.

"You two know each other?"

Her smile grew wider. "My ex," she said. "He is jealous."

I shrugged. I wasn't sure what was going on but I did not think that Celim Bakar was jealous, or at least not very jealous.

"Let us find a table and sit down," Diamond said. "I wish to know you better."

She took my hand and pulled me along to a dark booth in the corner. We placed our drinks down on the table. She leaned close, rubbed her breasts against my chest and licked my ear. I drew a deep breath. "I am not wearing anything under my skirt," she whispered. "Touch me."

My nostrils flared. I could smell her arousal, and something else. I reached down under her skirt. Her folds were slick and she caught her breath. I grinned and inserted a finger. She gasped and spread her legs wider. I pushed the finger a little deeper, moved it back and forth. "Use two fingers," she whispered. I took my finger out, placed it under my nose and sniffed; at least three different alkaloids along with her own scent.

There was a word for what she was, *Venefica*, I think, poison woman. In ancient Rome, they took young girls and fed them small doses of poison until they became immune to the poison, and then they slowly, steadily increased the dose until their bodies were imbued with it. The Venefica were weapons. Anyone who had sex with them would die.

I didn't think that they wanted me to die. It would be too suspicious, too obvious. Gath would lose face. One of the alkaloids that I smelled was the same one my brother Jimmy had asked me to sample, back at his bar. Hallucinogenic, not addictive and relatively short-acting, but then, there were three distinct scents…they meant to drug me. They wanted me to be sluggish, hung over and slow. They wanted me to lose.

I looked at Diamond and grinned. She was so very beautiful. "Let us go upstairs," she whispered. "I want to be alone with you."

"Alright," I said. "Yes, that's a very good idea."

Flickering candles lit the room. The carpets were deep, the walls and ceiling covered in mirrors. The bed was plush, soft and wide. Diamond kissed me as soon as we walked in, her tongue probing my mouth. I kissed her back. "Let me undress you," she said.

I grinned. "Let's undress each other," I said, and we did, caressing and nibbling on each inch of skin as it became exposed. Soon we were lying naked on the bed, her body twined around mine. I held her close, her back pressed against my chest, one hand caressing her nipples. "You're so beautiful," I whispered.

41

"I want you," she said. "Enter me from behind."

I smiled, cupped her breasts, squeezed softly, reached up further with my hands and pressed on both carotid arteries. She gasped. "Yes," I whispered, and squeezed. "Yes."

She drew a great, shuddering breath. Her body trembled. "Oh," I gasped. "Oh." I moved back and forth, panted, shuddered and groaned. Then I rolled over on my back, sighing. "You are absolutely wonderful," I whispered. "I could make love to you forever."

She didn't answer. She was unconscious. "Diamond?" I shook her gently. "Wake up."

She stirred and gave a little groan. "Too much to drink," I muttered. "Ah, well..."

I got out of bed, found my clothes scattered around the room and put them back on. I moved slowly and staggered a little, shaking my head, pretending that the drugs in Diamond's body were starting to affect me. I leaned over and kissed her on the forehead. "Sleep well," I whispered for the benefit of those who I knew were watching. "You're amazing. You're absolutely fantastic."

Ten minutes later, I found my guards, glumly waiting for me by the bar, drinking water and resenting it. "Let's get out of here," I said. "I've had enough for one night."

On the way toward the door, we passed Celim Bakar, sitting with a small group of men. He looked grim but his eyes lit up when he saw me. He saluted me with his glass as we passed. I winked at him and he nodded back, smiling.

Interesting, I thought. Very interesting.

Chapter 7

"The political situation here is more complicated than we realized. There are factions." We had the morning to rest, thank God. Captain Jones, Commander Boyd and I were sitting in the *Endeavor*'s control room. Low intensity lasers constantly licked at our ship. The lasers could detect minute vibrations and presumably allowed Gath to listen in to our conversations. We played an innocuous tape of mundane chatter to distract them while the three of us sat in a shielded room near the center of the ship.

"The majority faction, the Interventionists, believe in world domination." Commander Boyd was looking at his screen, frowning as he spoke. "They're convinced that they have a destiny to rule all the inferior races. They consider themselves the legitimate heirs to the First Empire and the only ones who've preserved the martial heritage of our illustrious ancestors."

Captain Jones rolled his eyes. The Commander grinned. "Yeah," he said. "I know."

"But they have opposition," I said.

"They do." He squinted at the screen. "Until about twenty years ago, Gath was a predominantly agrarian society with a large but basically low-tech military. A lot of nomadic herders. The land is fertile but winters in the north are harsh. Almost thirty percent of the population migrates with the seasons, going south when the weather grows cold and moving back up with the reindeer herds in Summertime.

"All of that changed when Atif Erdogan came to power."

I knew this, of course. Gath had been a society dominated by its elders in a limited form of democracy. In order to vote, you had to be over fifty years old and own property, not necessarily land; a herd of reindeer would do, anything that gave you a stake in the outcome. Such systems are generally conservative. Decisions tend to be made slowly, after much consideration and debate.

Atif Erdogan was fifty-five years old when he was elected to be head of the ruling Presidium. He quickly moved to replace retiring government ministers with his own adherents. A threat developed over a disputed border with Serevak, their neighbor to the north and the Presidium voted Erdogan executive powers in order to respond. The executive powers were never rescinded. At the same time, Erdogan encouraged the development of a more advanced technological base. The economy improved. Luxury goods, while still not common, became more available. Erdogan was popular. After ten years, his real agenda became apparent, or perhaps he changed his views. Who can say? In any case, the Interventionists slowly grew in power and when Erdogan died, his hand- picked successor, Idris Kartal, took over.

"A backlash has been developing. Despite the news blackout, these people are not completely isolated from the world. They are aware of outside events and what happened in Meridien was too much to swallow for at least some of them. I mean, most don't care. Many approve but a significant number understand the implications. They don't want to be at war with the world. The Conservative faction has been growing.

"Nasim Bakar won the grand tournament five years ago. He's popular and he currently leads the Conservatives."

"Celim Bakar's brother," I said.

Commander Boyd nodded. "Yes."

"Great," I said. "That's just great."

The final challenge of the games was a trek across two hundred kilometers of wilderness, basically a much larger version of the obstacle course. We all wore Gathian Wayfarer uniforms with the insignia removed, light, comfortable and tough, able to withstand a lot of punishment. We were issued a knife, a canteen and a tube of iodine tablets to purify drinking water, and that was it.

Scoring of the trek was complicated. The time you took to reach the finish line counted, of course, but it was less than fifty percent of the total. Points were awarded for overcoming obstacles, for ingenuity, for avoiding injury. You were expected to do more than merely survive. In order to win this phase of the competition, you were required to prevail. There could be only one overall winner but cooperation with your fellow contestants did receive points. You also received points for eliminating competition.

Fighting with each other was not allowed for the first hour of the trek. After that, it was no holds barred. We could all calculate the odds. Like chess, the endgame becomes easier as pieces are removed from the board. We were dropped off one-by-one, a few hundred yards apart.

The truck slowed to a stop, I jumped off and started running. I didn't see any of the others at first and that was fine by me. I had twenty kilometers of grassland to get through before I reached a range of foothills. The grassland was inhabited by modified buffalo, smaller than ancient Earth bison but occasionally aggressive. I could smell a small herd in the distance and another off to my left. I circled around them both, adding some time to the run but avoiding possible trouble.

Suddenly, I stopped; a strange scent on the air, not a scent that I recognized, pungent and rank and straight ahead of me. The grass wasn't high enough to block my vision, just high enough to make running difficult. And then something stood up. I didn't know what it was, exactly, some sort of modified bear. It wasn't quite as tall as me but was much wider and heavier and no doubt much stronger. It saw me, opened its mouth, roared and charged. The knife was in my hand before I even thought about it and as the bear thing came toward me, I dropped, rolled to the side and swiped at the Achilles tendon of its left leg. It roared louder, and in the distance, something just like it roared back.

I flipped to my feet and ran. Nothing can run with a slashed Achilles tendon. The thing roared in rage and it tried to lumber after me but its roaring grew fainter as I gained distance and I soon left it behind.

Whatever it was, it was nothing that I had ever heard of or read about, some deliberate mutation or perhaps something exotic purchased from offworld.

I crossed a small ditch and saw a stand of trees in the distance: an oasis. We had been shown maps of the course. I knew where I was. The oasis contained a small water hole and I couldn't go a full three days without water. They gave us a canteen but we were required to find our own water.

There is a curious sort of mutual agreement that takes place among animals in the wilderness. Every living thing needs water and water can be hard to come by. Lions truly do lie down with lambs (goats, actually, and small deer and gazelles) by a water hole in the wilderness. The grass was greener near the water. Shrubs and flowering plants grew in the sunshine. A small fish jumped in the pond. A wading bird looked at me, curious, but otherwise ignored me. Two buffalo grazed stolidly and a large feline with spots on its sides lazily brushed a fly off its fur with its tail and yawned as I walked up to the bank.

I kneeled, filled the canteen and put in an iodine tab. It would be safe to drink in thirty minutes.

I frowned. A few meters away, grass was piled behind a boulder. One of my fellow contestants was hiding under the grass. I could smell him.

He was quick and almost silent but I was ready when he came at me. I whirled, his knife passing over my head. I dropped below his swing, continued with my turn and planted my own knife in his abdomen, all the way to the hilt. I twisted, pulled and watched as his guts and a fountain of blood slid out and dripped wetly to the ground. He looked at me with disbelief.

"What did you expect, moron?" I asked.

His lips trembled. He tried to say something but then the breath gurgled in his throat and he collapsed and didn't move again.

I recognized him. His name was Berat Feyyaz. He was twenty-five years old and had a mother and two sisters. I had noticed him last night at Club Menagerie, sitting with a group of friends, looking like he hadn't a care in the world…and now he was dead because I had killed him. Of course, he had tried to kill me first. All fair enough, I suppose, but it still felt wrong.

The oasis was silent. All the animals, the big cat, the two buffalo, even the bird were looking at me. Overhead, three buzzards already circled in lazy arcs. I shrugged and left his body for the scavengers to take care of. I tried to ignore the cameras planted in the trees and the drone flying overhead, transmitting everything that happened for the entertainment of the world.

I went on.

Chapter 8

I made good progress in the foothills but the trail soon grew steep and it narrowed as the hills gave way to a range of low mountains. A rumble of thunder sounded in the distance and the sun turned into a dimmer orange ball as haze and then clouds began to obscure it. Shadows lengthened. Evening was coming on and I was hungry. I had grabbed a handful of berries and some edible ferns growing alongside the trail but I would lose too much time if I stopped to forage. I needed protein.

I didn't think food would be much a problem, though, not for me, and as the evening turned into night, I was proven correct. Most of the birds had returned to their nests. Squirrels and rabbits cowered in their burrows, hiding from the owls, the lynx and the snakes.

None of them could hide from my augmented senses. The night grew cool and the heat signature emitted by living bodies shone brightly in my sight. A bird's nest hidden in some brush gave me three eggs. I ate them raw, sucking them out of the shell as I walked on, and I finished the berries that I had picked up earlier.

Anything tastes good if you're starving but I decided to give a pass to the slugs and the insects. It might come to that in the end but I wasn't hungry enough yet for the more exotic options and I hoped that I never would be.

Another rumble of thunder stopped me. The night was growing colder and I had no desire to be wandering around in the rain. Time to seek shelter. I found some dried branches, about two meters in length, tied them together with small vines, forming open rectangles, then covered the rectangles with sheets of bark that I stripped from trees. I placed the resulting panels against a rock outcropping, giving me a crude but functional lean-to. One piece of wood had a larger diameter than the others. I hefted it in my hand, liking the weight.

The rain was steady. I wasn't going anywhere until it stopped and I had all night. I crouched down in the lean-to, took out my knife, picked up a sharp piece of rock and began to carve. I soon had a deep groove in the wood and a modified handle on one end. Another small tree branch fit snugly into the groove: an atlatl—a primitive spear thrower, and a spear, with a blunt, rounded end that would also serve as a staff. You never know when a staff, a spear and a spear thrower might come in handy. I took a few minutes more to sharpen one end of the improvised spear and tucked them both into a corner of the lean-to.

A pile of soft leaves served as a bed and I closed my eyes as the rain continued to fall. It had been an eventful day, but a depressing one. I hoped that tomorrow would be more boring. Sometimes, I thought, boring is good. Finally, I dropped into a fitful sleep.

Birds chirping over my head woke me a few hours later. I was still tired and sluggish but I couldn't afford to waste any more time. Dawn was starting to break and the rain had passed on by. I needed to be on the move. Too bad that I couldn't bring the lean-to but I had no way to carry it. I tied the spear and the atlatl to my back with some vines, checked to make sure that I could move my arms freely and then started jogging.

Within an hour, I came to a small canyon. Trees clung to the steep walls but it didn't take long to climb down to the bottom and then back up the other side. A few kilometers further on, the ground grew soft, and soon after, it turned into a swamp. I probed the sodden mud with my new staff, avoiding the softest parts of it but soon came to open water. I considered my options and didn't like any of them, then shrugged, and waded out.

I was halfway across when I saw a wake slowly coming toward me. I looked at it and groaned. Alligators were uncommon here. We were close to the Southern end of their range, but it appeared that I was out of luck. I stood very still as the wake came closer. It wasn't a big one, just big enough to have no fear of men. It came faster at the end, reared up out of the water and opened its jaws wide. I jammed the spear into its mouth and pushed back. It thrashed its tail and rolled over but I stayed on top of it, shoving the sharpened end down its throat. I rose up and pressed with all my weight, forcing the gator against the bottom. The spear went deeper and the reptile's struggles grew frantic but I held on and after a few minutes, they slowly ceased.

Food. I smiled and dragged it to the opposite bank by its tail.

It isn't hard to make a fire if you have a built-in source of electricity. I touched the tip of my knife to a small pile of dry leaves and shot a jolt of current down the blade. The leaves smoked and quickly caught. I piled on some small sticks, then a few larger ones and in less than a minute I had a good blaze going. I cut off the gator's tail and skinned it, carved out the tenderloins from the carcass, hung the meat on some sharpened sticks and broiled it over the flames. It wasn't too hard to improvise a bag with some large leaves and a few pieces of vine and soon I was back on the trail, feeling pretty good about the day, so far.

Thankfully, the ground began to rise again and finally, I left the swamp behind. I made good time for about twenty kilometers, chewing on a piece of cold alligator as I jogged along the trail. Not the best meat I had ever tasted but not the worst, either. A little salt would have helped.

I stopped. The birds had stopped singing. Never a good sign. I sniffed. Rich earth, loam, turned over dirt and somewhere, faintly, the scent of a human. No...I sniffed again—four humans. Not too close to me, not yet. I climbed a tree. From ten meters up, it wasn't hard to see them. They had dug a pit across the trail and covered it with a layer of fallen leaves, probably over a woven frame, and probably there would be sharpened stakes at the bottom. Four men crouched behind trees, waiting. Three carried spears; one with a stone point lashed to the shaft. The fourth held a crudely improvised bow.

What to do? I sat in my tree and considered the question. Points would be awarded for confronting them but that would only help me if I lived through the confrontation. I was tempted. I didn't know these people but I knew that I didn't like them. I'm prejudiced that way.

"*Psst*," I looked down. Peering up at me through the leaves was the smiling face of Celim Bakar. His hands were empty and spread to the sides. He stood there, posture quite deliberately not threatening. I scanned the area around the tree. He was alone.

"Come down," he whispered. "We should talk."

Why not? At the moment, it was four against one. A little cooperation seemed like a good thing.

A few minutes later, we were sitting next to each other on a fallen log. "Alligator?" I asked.

He smiled. "No, thank you. I killed a small gazelle and smoked the meat. I have enough to last until the end of the contest."

"Would you like to trade some?"

He appeared to think about it. "No," he said, "but thank you."

I wondered how he had made a fire. That old rubbing two sticks together routine is a lot harder than it seems. And I really would have preferred some gazelle meat to the rest of the alligator. "How do you know Diamond?" I asked.

"Diamond?"

"The woman at Menagerie. You warned me about her."

"Ah. Elena," he said. "We were in the Junior guard together. She was ambitious."

I had to smile. *Ambitious.* "Yes, I could see that about her."

"I'm glad that you survived. Some don't."

"I understand," I said. "What can I do for you, then?"

He looked away, frowned. "There were twenty-five of us left before the trek began. I had the most points but that no longer matters. We are all close enough so that whoever wins the trek will win the tournament."

I nodded. "Fewer than twenty-five by now," I said. "One of them tried to kill me and I killed him instead. I'm sure there are others. You remove a few pieces from the board and the odds in your favor improve."

Celim Bakar winced and seemed genuinely distressed. "Winning brings fame and glory. Most of them do not think beyond this." He shook his head. "They are young."

"Fame, glory, unlimited breeding rights and an appointment to the Presidium," I pointed out, "which includes a vote on every action that your nation takes. Power."

"Yes," he said.

"And which of these things motivates you?"

"Unlike most of my people, I have studied our history. The First Empire was the ultimate power in this galaxy for over four thousand years, and it is gone as if it had never existed. Power is an illusion, in the end. Nobody keeps power forever."

"Four thousand years might as well be forever, for most of us. More often than not, kings and Imperators die in bed."

"Bah." He grimaced. "My people would never tolerate a king. Most kings were congenital morons. No, we are given power for a short period of time only, and then it is somebody else's turn to make decisions." He shook his head. "'*Think, in this batter'd Caravanserai, Whose Portals are alternate Night and Day, How Sultan after Sultan with his Pomp, Abode his hour or two, And went his way.*'" He shook his head again and sighed.

Celim Bakar was an interesting fellow. "Omar Khayyam?"

"Yes. Omar Khayyam's poetry tends to dwell on the themes of futility, acceptance, making the best of each moment, and transience. He was a wise man."

"So again, which of these things motivates you?"

"The survival of my people is what motivates me," he said.

I pondered that. Celim Bakar's concerns were legitimate. One cannot reveal what one does not know and the crew of the *Endeavor* had deliberately been kept in the dark regarding Meridien's preparations and ideas regarding either retaliation or pre-emption. We did not know what might be happening back home and we certainly did not know what the governments of Meridien and our allied nations might be planning, but it seemed certain that none of it boded well for the future of Gath. "I think you're right to be worried," I said.

He looked at me. "Will you help me?"

And there it was. I had been given a mission: to make Gath look ridiculous, to weaken Gath's morale and to give heart to Gath's enemies, to beat them at their own game. And yet it is said that no plan survives contact with the enemy. Celim Bakar presented an unexpected opportunity—maybe. "Help you how?" I asked.

He drew in a deep breath. "If we continue on this course, you and I will fight. We will have to. Maybe you can beat me." He shrugged. "I don't think you can, but you have done very well in the games so far and I would be foolish to deny the possibility."

"You're asking me to let you win," I said.

He shook his head. "I'm asking you to help me win."

"Why should I?"

"You came with a military escort. You're not here as a private citizen. Would your nation be better served by your victory in these games or by a change in my government's policies?"

And there it was. I sat back on my log and considered. The patterns here could play out in so many different ways. "I need to think about this," I finally said. "Meanwhile, we both need to get to the finish line. For now, let's work together. We can fight later, if that's what we decide to do."

"Then swear it," he said. "Swear that you will abide by your word. Swear that you will not betray me."

I frowned. "Why would you take my word?"

He gave me a hard smile. "I always know when people are telling me the truth," he said. "It's a gift."

Again, Celim Bakar surprised me. I looked at him and smiled back. "I also know when people are telling me the truth."

He raised an eyebrow. "Really?"

I nodded. "Yes."

"Then we will both swear. Neither will betray the other. We will work together until the end. If you decide that we must fight, you will tell me and it will be at the finish line, in the eyes of the world. I swear this to you."

"Yes," I said. "I agree."

"Good." He drew a deep breath, then turned to the woods at our side and said, "Janelle, come out."

I knew she was there, of course. I had been waiting to see what she would do. The bushes rustled and the brunette amazon who had beaten Jennifer in the knife tournament stepped into our small clearing. She was as tall as me and if you liked them muscled and tough, one of the most beautiful women I have ever seen. Her hair was black, thick and braided, and hung down to her waist. Her shoulders were broad, her waist thin. A narrow white scar went from below one ear to the corner of her mouth and she had two spears tied across her back. She looked at me with suspicion and said something in her own language to Celim Baker.

"This is not courteous behavior," he said to her. "This man is now our ally. We will speak so that he can understand us."

She frowned, then gave a little shrug. "If you betray us, I will kill you slowly," she said.

I laughed. I couldn't help it. "Yes, of course," I said. "I would expect nothing less."

Her eyes narrowed and I thought for a moment that she would attack me but then she gave a reluctant smile. "That did sound a little silly, didn't it?"

"But very sincere." I smiled. "Before we go any further, I think that Janelle should swear as well."

She shrugged and did so and then sat next to Celim Bakar on his log. Almost absently, he put his arm around her shoulder and hugged her close to his side. "What is our plan?" she asked.

"Simple enough," I said. "There are four of them and three of us but we have the advantage of surprise. Let's take them."

"I like simple plans," she said.

Celim Bakar frowned, looking pensive. "Yes," he said. "I agree."

Chapter 9

We could have simply circled around through the woods and gone on but that would have left them free to assassinate the next contestant who came down the trail, which somehow bothered all three of us; and anyway, meeting adversity and overcoming it would give us points.

We did circle around but only until we were right behind them, slipping soundlessly through the shadows, almost close enough to reach out and touch them. Celim Bakar nodded his head and we exploded. He jumped on the one with the bow, put a knee in the middle of his back, grabbed his head and wrenched it to the side. The archer's neck cracked and he fell, dead before he touched the ground.

I took the one with the stone spear point. It wasn't pretty or elegant. I jammed my own spear in his back and he fell, screaming. Then I did what Celim Bakar had done, I crouched over him and twisted his neck until it broke.

Janelle had a little more difficulty. Her target had enough warning to turn and raise his weapon. She aimed a kick at his groin but he jerked to the side, enough to partially deflect the kick. He grunted as her foot slammed into his thigh. He completed a turn and aimed a kick of his own at her head. She moved in under his guard and slammed her knee into his face. His nose crunched and he fell to the ground, still breathing but unconscious.

By this time, Celim Bakar and I had moved on the fourth man. He looked wildly back and forth, then dropped his spear, turned, and ran. Celim Bakar hefted his own spear, as if thinking of throwing it, then shrugged. "Let him go," he said. "He's lost. He has no chance of winning the tournament."

"Unless he creeps back and kills us while we're sleeping," Janelle said. "Then he might win."

I shrugged. "Small odds of that. We'll be looking for him to try."

Her posture indicated that she did not entirely agree with me but she said nothing more and tied up the unconscious one with some vines. "They'll free him when the contest is over. Unless another contestant comes along and decides to slit his throat."

Celim Bakar and I looked at each other. I shook my head. Definitely not our problem. "You don't get any points for killing a restrained contestant. Let's get going," he said.

The next few kilometers were uneventful. Night fell but both moons were bright. We slowed our pace but kept moving until close to midnight, then came upon a grassy clearing with a small stream. "Stop for the night?" I said.

Celim and Janelle looked at each other. Some wordless communication took place then they both moved to the edge of the clearing and began to gather leaves. The night was warm enough and the sky was clear. There was no need to make a shelter. "I'll take the first watch," I said. Celim and Janelle lay down on their pile of leaves and were soon asleep. The night remained quiet and nothing approached us. After three hours, I stood a few feet away from Celim and poked him with my spear. He came awake instantly, knife in his fist, then grinned and rose soundlessly to his feet. I laid my head down on the soft pile of leaves and fell into grateful oblivion.

Morning found us back on the trail. The sun was shining but it wasn't too hot and the air smelled fresh. The first few hours were thankfully uneventful and we made good time. "This will be over soon," Celim Bakar said to me as we walked. "Have you given any thought to my request?"

I frowned. Truthfully, I had thought of little else. "I'm still thinking," I said.

He nodded, and left me alone.

The trail narrowed and soon we were forced to go single file, Janelle first, then Celim and then me. A few kilometers further on, Janelle stopped. "Something's wrong," she said. I had been aware of it for some time, a faint, acrid smell, unlike anything I had ever known. Unfortunately, it was growing stronger as we neared the end of the trek.

"There is a clearing up ahead," Celim said to me.

"Leading to a stone embankment that contains the entrance to a series of caves," I said.

We had all memorized the map. Janelle bit her lip. Celim frowned. Many animals used caves for shelter.

"The finish line is just beyond the caves," Janelle said. "We have to go through the clearing."

Celim shook his head. "I'm tired of this. Let's get it over with."

We were young, strong, fast and physically fit. There wasn't much on this world that should be able to intimidate the three of us, but then again, discretion may or may not be the better part of valor but it won't get you killed. Finally, I shrugged. Fuck it. I was tired of this, too. "Yeah," I said. "Let's do it."

Celim nodded. Janelle still looked worried. "Men," she muttered, and Celim grinned at her.

The trail was too obvious and too exposed. We split up, got down on our stomachs and wriggled forward through the underbrush. Soon, I was crouched on the edge of the clearing, which was surrounded on each side by rocky cliffs, turning the whole thing into a sort of amphitheater, or a trap.

A few seconds later, I could see Celim and then Janelle's face a few meters away, heads barely visible against the vegetation. Bones lay on the floor of the clearing. Many bones. Across from us, the trail continued through a narrow passage. A meter or so away from the trail, a dark cave opening loomed in the cliffs.

Despite our eagerness to go on, we weren't insane. We waited and we watched and half an hour later another contestant walked down the trail behind us. I smiled. It was the fourth member of the group who had tried to ambush us the day before, the one who got away. Apparently, he had recovered his spear, or made a new one. As I looked at him, I wondered how he had gotten this far. He was loud, for one thing. He made no attempt at all to walk silently. Sticks and dried leaves crunched under his feet. He was tall and thin and didn't appear very formidable.

I had watched him fight, though. He was fast and a lot stronger than he appeared. He knew what he was doing in the octagon, but out here? I shrugged. There had to be more to him than we could see.

He blundered past us into the clearing, then stopped and frowned down at the bones. Something stirred in the cave opening and then emerged. "Oh, shit," I whispered silently.

Many thousands of years ago, there lived in Southeast Asia a species of giant ape called *Gigantopithecus,* the largest primate ever known. It stood over three meters tall, weighed over 500 kilos, ate primarily fruit and was related to the orangutan.

This thing was bigger, not taller but broader across the shoulders and enormous through the chest. It crawled out of the cave mouth, unfolded to its full height, glared at the tiny human that had dared to invade its domain, and roared. It didn't look like an orangutan, more like a mutated gorilla. Judging from all the bones, I didn't think it ate fruit.

The sound was overwhelming. All around us, the jungle grew silent. The man stared at it but strangely, he grinned. He pulled the spear from his back, held it in front of him in guard position and said, "Come on, you ugly bastard. It's time to die."

I looked over at Celim. He raised his eyebrows and shrugged. Janelle stared at the thing, her face white.

The ape stopped roaring and what might have been a smile crossed its face. It shuffled forward. The man stood his ground, smiling. The ape seemed in no hurry. Within a second, it loomed over the puny human and his insignificant looking spear. It cocked its head to the side, inspecting its prey, then it raised both hands over its head and brought them down.

The man was no longer there. He was fast, very fast, with augmented speed and reflexes. Suddenly, he stood next to the ape and thrust his spear toward its belly. The ape turned and the spear grazed its side, opening a shallow cut and then the ape snatched the spear away, held it in its hands and snapped it like a twig. The man stared, turned to run and suddenly, the giant ape was holding him by both shoulders, three meters off the ground, staring into his face. The man snarled and reached his arms out to both sides of the ape's head. A snapping sound and a bright blue burst of electricity erupted from the man's fingers. The ape roared again, even louder than before. It staggered but didn't let go. Then suddenly the man's head was between the ape's enormous teeth. It crunched down. Blood fountained up from the man's neck. His decapitated body twitched, once, twice, then slumped lifelessly in the gigantic ape's arms. The ape's teeth moved back and forth, grating on bone. It spat out a piece of skull, swallowed the rest of the head and taking the body with him, crawled back into its cave.

"That's our cue," I said.

Janelle nodded. We ran across the clearing, back onto the trail and didn't stop until we had put the cave and its enormous guardian far behind us.

The finish line was concealed within a stone arch lined with flowers on both sides. We looked at it. Celim Bakar stood next to me, arms crossed in front of his chest, his face impassive. A scoreboard containing all the rankings was set up next to the arch. Celim Bakar's name was still listed first but I was second, only a few points behind. Janelle was fifth.

I liked Celim Bakar, and I admired him. He was smart, strong, honest and loyal. He stood there, waiting, asking for no quarter, ready to accept whatever decision I made. He was bigger than me and he was stronger. I thought I was a touch faster but I had a weapon that he lacked, two weapons, actually. I had seen his face when the ape killed his last victim. Celim had been both surprised and amazed at the electricity the man could generate. I had the same ability. Celim, apparently did not. And there was also the retractable claw in each index finger, which connected to small glands in my palm that manufactured a nerve poison, similar to cobra venom. If I flexed my hand just the right way, the claw would extend.

I looked down at my open palm, flexed my fingers, smiled to myself and shook my head. In the end, I had a mission. That mission was to advance the interests of my nation and I had come to the conclusion that giving a seat in the government of Gath to Celim Bakar, a national hero inclined to favor peace over war was more important than my own ego.

"Let's walk through together," I said.

I could see Janelle suddenly relax and she gave a tiny, shaky nod. Celim regarded me impassively. "Very well," he said. "You have been a good companion."

And so we did. It was pretty anti-climactic, in the end. There weren't any cheering crowds nor waving banners. We walked under the arch together, the three of us linking arms. Two judges impassively noted our times into the scoreboard.

Twelve competitors were dead but six remained out on the course and it was at least barely possible that one or more of them could still beat Celim's total score. They showed us to a tent where a feast was laid out on a buffet table. I walked over to a trash can and dumped the remains of the alligator then I picked up a plate and began filling it. Janelle and Celim did the same. We sat together at a table and waited for the contest to be over.

"So, assuming you win," I said to Celim, "what will you do with your unlimited breeding rights?"

Janelle narrowed her eyes. "He will have his babies with me."

Celim rolled his eyes but gave her an indulgent smile. He continued to eat, shoveling food into his mouth with metronomic regularity.

"All of them?"

They were sitting very close together, comfortable with each other. "All of them," she said.

"Seems a waste," I said.

She grinned. "I shall keep him occupied."

I smiled. Janelle was quite a woman. I didn't doubt her.

All six remaining contestants had to cross the giant ape's territory. Three died. Two more staggered in, one after the other, nursing minor injuries. The last managed to get past the ape's enclosure but could not continue. He collapsed a kilometer from the finish line with a broken arm and a severed brachial artery. The overall scores did not change significantly and two hours later, Celim Bakar was crowned the grand champion of the games.

The awards were given out by a man named Atif Ferrara, Foreign Minister in the administration of Idris Kartal. I received a plaque for my second-place finish and a large sum of money and was invited to participate again in five year's time. Atif Ferrara gave me a smile that might have looked friendly to the cameras and shook my hand, almost like he meant it.

"Thank you, sir," I said. "I'm looking forward to trying again."
Fat chance, I thought. *Fat fucking, bloody chance.*

Janelle finished fifth overall, and first among the women. She was also given a large monetary prize and an invitation to repeat her performance. She stared at Ferrara, who blinked his eyes and dropped her hand quickly. She smiled, leaned toward him and whispered something too low for the microphones to pick up. I saw his face grow pale.

Yes, indeed, I thought. She was quite a woman, that Janelle. She and Celim Bakar made an impressive couple.

Oh, was I looking forward to going home. I had had more than enough of the hospitality of Gath.

Chapter 10

"Shielded," Captain Jones said. "There are only two places in the city we haven't been able to penetrate. This is one of them."

Our recorders, almost as light as air, had drifted on the wind and settled over much of the city. In the three weeks since our arrival they had collected data and sent it into cyberspace, billions of bytes, millions of images and sounds. I had paid little attention to it all, being engrossed in the Grand Tournament but the Tournament was over now and this, after all, was the game that counted.

It was once said of ancient Russia that on her borders, she could have only enemies and vassals. Gath was the same. Perhaps the foremost military power on the continent, her neighbors uniformly feared her. Gath had no real allies and an economy dependent upon the export of produce, raw materials and easily derived pharmaceuticals. Gath received a small amount of capital from the licensing of the games and the minimal amount of tourism that the games generated but compared to their national budget, it was a pittance. Economic sanctions imposed on Gath after their attempted subversion of Meridien were beginning to bite.

In addition, the cold war was starting to turn hot. Three Gath ships had been boarded at sea and their cargo confiscated. Gath airships were no longer welcome in most nations on the continent. Smugglers attempting to bring goods into Gath's cities were being intercepted. The cost of survival was rising.

The Presidium and the ruling council were aware, of course. Nothing was publicly admitted but the citizenry seemed to realize that something was up. Rumors were flying and unrest was stirring. Nasim Bakar, Celim Bakar's brother, had given a speech to the ruling council. It was scathing, making reference to tyrants and empires throughout history and the bloody end to which all had ultimately come. Idris Kartal, the Presidium's Chief, had sat and listened with an attentive smile and after, he had called his most trusted adherents into his private office, which was five stories under the ground, equipped with a negative pressure air system and swept and vacuumed daily. Our recorders had not been able to penetrate below the third level. Nevertheless, it could be seen that General Ferrara and his fellow Interventionists had emerged pleased from this meeting. When the General returned to his office, he called in his subordinates. We were able to record this meeting and we didn't like it.

"Not unexpected," Captain Jones said.

I nodded. "What is the second place that you haven't been able to penetrate?" I said.

The Captain frowned. "Here," he said, and pointed to a mansion surrounded by trees and a high stone wall. Armed troops patrolled the grounds at all times.

"Why not?"

"Our bugs short out. The place is surrounded by an energy shield."

We had such shields, of course. The First Empire could supposedly tailor them at will. Meridien's, and our allies' as well, were all spherical, surrounding a central generator. They were much better for airships than for buildings, since ground resistance quickly sapped their energy, but somehow, Gath had the technology to maintain such a shield. That was ominous. I wondered what else they had.

I looked at the photographs for a long time, assessing potential weak points, of which there seemed to be none and then shrugged. "First things first," I said. "This place will still be there."

It is said that those who do evil must do so in the dark. Not entirely true, of course. Absolute power means you can do anything that you want, with no fear at all of who might be looking. I was banking on the fact that Idris Kartal did not have absolute power, and I planned on staying in well lit places. Being a newly minted celebrity helped.

That evening, a small crowd of admirers followed me down the street, curious as to where I was going. Jennifer clung to my arm, wearing an indulgent but faintly disapproving smile. She spread her hands to the side and gestured at my back as if asking, "What can I do with him?" The crowd loved it.

I had wandered from bar to bar, buying drinks and publicly celebrating my excellent showing in the Grand Tournament, and the citizens of Gath seemed happy to help me do it. It was now late at night. I waved my bottle, staggered a little, walked up the steps of Celim Bakar's spacious mansion and knocked on the door. "Hey," I roared. "Let me in! I have something for you!"

The door opened. Two large men in Gath military uniforms, armed with short swords and rifles, stood in the doorway. They didn't look happy to see me. I smiled at them. "Is Celim at home? I have a present for him." One of them gave me a disdainful look and said something to the other in his own language. The second guard turned without a word and vanished back inside. A few seconds later, Celim and Janelle stood in the doorway. They looked at me. Celim blinked, stared at the crowd and gave Jennifer a cautious nod. Janelle clucked her tongue. "You better come in," she said. They both waved and smiled at the crowd, who snapped pictures and waved back at their conquering heroes. The last guard stepped to the side but stayed close.

I staggered in, almost falling on the front steps. Jennifer followed sedately, flashing one last embarrassed smile to the crowd as she entered. Then the door closed. I straightened, drew a deep breath and grinned at them both. "Is this place secure?" I asked.

"Entirely," Celim said. He turned to the guard and said, "Stand down." The guard gave Celim a military salute, turned on his heel and left without looking back.

A small hallway led into a cavernous living room with a dark, stone floor covered with rugs, low chairs, couches and carved wooden tables, a colorful, comfortable room. "Come," Celim Bakar said. "Sit."

I was scanning the place for bugs. I didn't see any. Jennifer and I both sat down opposite Celim and Janelle. Janelle gave Jennifer a long look. "I know you," she said.

"This is Jennifer Mallet," I said. "Celim Bakar and Janelle." I frowned. "I never did get your last name."

She glanced at Celim. "Madarik," she said. "Soon, it will be Bakar." She turned back to Jennifer. "When we fought in the circle, you let me win. Why?"

I looked at Jennifer. This was news to me. She gave a tiny shrug. "I didn't let you win. I may have held back, just a little."

"Why?"

"It seemed prudent."

"Why?" she asked again.

"We're leaving soon but you'll still be here." Jennifer grinned and glanced at me. "I had enough foresight to look up my competitors. Your father and your fiancé"—she nodded at Celim—"are both prominent members of the Conservationists. We're on the same side. I thought that you needed a victory more than I did."

We all stared at Jennifer. Finally, I cleared my throat and turned to Celim. "We wanted to let you know that your brother is going to be arrested."

"You know this for a fact?" Celim asked.

"Yes."

Celim sat back, thought about it for a moment then shrugged. "This is not a surprise. We've been expecting it." He smiled wolfishly. "I will be taking my seat on the council in a week. Our faction is growing stronger every day. Soon, we will have enough votes to stop this madness."

"If they let you live long enough to vote."

"They will not find us to be easy prey." He gave me a lazy grin. "My brother is already in a safe place. For the past month, most of his public appearances have been carried out by a stand-in."

I pondered this. "You know your own business," I said. "Good luck."

"Thank you," he said. "Your people should leave while they still can."

"Yes," I said. "We intend to. We're leaving at dawn."

Chapter 11

We did plan on leaving at dawn but Captain Jones called me up to the bridge shortly before midnight. "Look," he said. "I think you'll find this interesting."

Our bugs had still not been able to penetrate the mansion's shielding but we had drones constantly watching the place. Over the past twelve hours, Idris Kartal and Atif Ferrara had been escorted in and spent approximately three hours before leaving. Then, a few hours after sundown, the front door opened and two men walked out. I stared at their faces. Captain Jones smiled at my reaction. The Captain had been thoroughly briefed on the events preceding the siege of Aphelion and he knew who these men were.

Derek Landry and Winston Smith.

"Where are they now?" I asked.

"Club Menagerie," he said.

I looked at him. "Let's go have some fun."

My near-victory in the Grand Tournament would be old news in a month's time but right now, I was a popular celebrity, all the more popular for not having stolen the prize from a favored son of Gath. Alten Deniz seemed surprised to see us but was happy to usher me in, along with my entourage, which consisted of Jennifer, Captain Jones and five troopers, all of us dressed to party. "Welcome," Alten Deniz said. "Welcome indeed. You grace our establishment with your presence." I could almost see him licking his lips while counting the credits that our visit would bring in.

Menagerie, like all business establishments in Gath, was owned by the State and it had its own security. Our escort of Gath plainclothes was told to wait for us in the courtyard. They weren't happy about it but that was not my problem.

I had wondered if the presence of the tournament contestants on my previous visit might have led to a larger crowd than usual but evidently not. The music tonight was just as loud, the crowd just as large and the dancers just as frantic. The joint was jumping, just what we had hoped for. We needed the cover.

We spread out. Jennifer and I wandered over to the bar for drinks, which we pretended to sip, then joined the crowd on the dance floor, then stood near a stage while a woman with almost unnatural endowments did a slow strip tease. I sniffed the air. Derek Landry and Winston Smith had been here but the scent was at least an hour old.

Alten Deniz stood near the front entrance, greeting a man and a woman. The man wore a general's uniform, the woman was beautiful, older than most of the crowd but still in her prime. She wore a gown. Alten Deniz bowed very low, shook the man's hand and whispered something in his ear. The woman allowed her eyes to wander over the room. She gave a small disdainful sniff. The General smiled and Alten Deniz conducted them both to an elevator, flanked by two large guards in formal dress.

There are exclusive clubs, and then there are more exclusive clubs. The crowd here was rather young, I thought. Callow. They were the children of important people but they weren't the important people.

"Mr. Deniz," I said. "I am not pleased with you."

He blinked. "This is unfortunate. We at Club Menagerie wish nothing more than the happiness of our guests."

"These people"—I waved my hand at the room—"are unsophisticated. I was expecting a more rarified form of entertainment from your establishment."

He stared at me, then a slow, crooked smile spread across his face. "My apologies," he said. "I didn't realize. Perhaps you might find what you are looking for in the more private and select areas of our establishment."

"Perhaps," I said.

His smile grew wider. "Please come with me."

I beckoned to Jennifer, who had a bemused expression on her face as she watched a contortionist on one of the stages. She nodded and silently took my arm. Alten Deniz gave us both a small bow, turned and conducted us to the elevator. "Feel free to avail yourselves of the amusements that you will find upstairs. They are less..."—he gave the room a quizzical smile before turning back toward Jennifer and I—"common than what is offered here."

"Thank you," I said. "That would be excellent."

He bowed again as the door closed.

"Private and select," Jennifer said.

"You heard? Private and select is just what we're looking for." I smiled at her. "Certainly not common."

She briefly raised her eyes to the ceiling and gave a tiny shrug.

The elevator doors opened and we exited into a small room covered in stone tiles, with low, soft furniture and colored tapestries hanging on the walls. The lights were dim, with small multi-colored bulbs twinkling in the corners. A hum of ventilation could not conceal the heavy scent of incense. Across from the elevator, three young women and one man sat on couches, passing a hookah back and forth, taking deep hits of fragrant smoke. One of the women giggled. Another moaned. The man looked back and forth between their faces, grinned and began to hum something low and atonal. The fourth woman lay back on the couch with her eyes closed and whispered, "Whoa..." to herself.

Jennifer frowned. "I guess that's fun," she said doubtfully.

The incense numbed my nose, and the acrid reek of the hookah made it worse. I sneezed, my eyes tearing. I could tell that Winston Smith and Derek Landry had been here. "Let's see what else is happening."

Three corridors led off from the first room. The first one led to a casino. I could see the general's beautiful companion pulling the arm of a slot machine. She pushed one token in after another, barely letting the reels stop spinning before popping in the next token. Her expression was blank. She did not look like she was enjoying herself.

Three roulette wheels occupied one corner of the room. Card tables and dice tables spread out across the floor. About half of the men wore military uniforms, none below the rank of Major. The women's fashions were up to date, except for the croupiers and waitresses, who wore nothing but g-strings and wide professional smiles. All of the women were beautiful.

Jennifer and I wandered around the room, curious. I stopped for a moment, threw a pair of dice, lost, shrugged and continued on. Nobody paid me the slightest attention, though a few of the men gave Jennifer speculative looks, which she ignored.

A polished wooden bar occupied one whole wall. I recognized a few of the bottles. They were all expensive and none of them were made in Gath. A few men and two women leaned on the bar, sipping drinks. They looked depressed. I guess they hadn't been winning. Derek Landry had stood there, not so long ago. Winston Smith as well, though his scent was fainter. The two men seemed to have split up once they arrived at the club.

We wandered down the corridor, following Landry's trail to a large open doorway that opened into what seemed at first glance to be another bar. It wasn't. Naked men and women, all young, all beautiful, lounged in the corners. Other men and women, guests of the club, would come up, converse for a few minutes and then would be conducted under an arch into another hallway with the companion of their choice. I glanced at Jennifer. She grinned. "It's one way to put yourself through collegium," she said.

"Landry is in there," I said.

"Good," she said. "Sooner or later, he'll come out."

"We can't hang around here without sampling the merchandise. It will look suspicious."

"You go on," she said. "I'll take care of it."

She had a grin on her face. That grin made me uncomfortable. "You're sure?"

"Leave Derek Landry to me."

I looked at her, uncertain. "Go on," she said. "Trust me," and she moved off to the bar, smiling.

Okay...

I stopped in a bathroom and put on a blonde wig, small lifts in my heels and some inserts above my gums that gave my face a fuller, more rounded look. Winston Smith wasn't likely to recognize me. I found him a few minutes later, sitting at a table behind an open door, playing some sort of card game. He was staring with fixed intensity at his cards, a small pile of chips sitting on the table in front of him. He didn't look happy. Good. I didn't want Winston Smith to be happy.

Ten chairs were set up around the walls. Three men sat and watched the game. I joined them, curious. The five men and one woman sitting around the table all knew each other. The stakes were high. I didn't understand how Smith, presumably the leader of a paramilitary hit team, could afford to play at this table. I found out quickly. I also found out that the name he was using was not Winston Smith—no surprise. The woman smiled at him, a very unpleasant smile, and said, "You're out of money. You owe me a forfeit, David."

He swallowed. Small beads of sweat covered his forehead. "I'll win it back," he said.

"Will you?" She shrugged. "Perhaps you will."

He didn't. He lost the next hand and the next.

"I think that's enough." The woman's smile was soft, cruel and triumphant. "I truly love it when you lose, David. You make the most wonderful sounds when I strap you to the table." She rose to her feet and held out a hand. "Come," she said. He swallowed but rose to his feet, swaying. Then he seemed to collect himself, straightened and followed the woman from the room. The other men looked at his retreating back. One man shook his head. Another shuddered. The rest merely smiled.

The woman was no longer young. She had red hair and a full, still voluptuous figure. She walked like she owned the place, or at least like she owned Winston Smith, who walked behind her with heavy, leaden steps. I held back and let them turn the corner before strolling from the room.

I followed their scent to a closed door at the end of a corridor. Similar rooms lined the hallway. I looked into one of them. A bare metal table stood in the center, with heavy leather straps at the hands, feet and chest. Metal cranks attached to each strap. A pulley stood above the table, presumably to suspend the victim in the air. Sharpened metal combs, small curved knives, lancets, finger and toe presses, and lead mallets hung on the walls. A small electric brazier stood next to the table with three iron rods of varying thickness sticking out of the top.

Winston Smith, I surmised, was in for an unpleasant time.

The walls were thick, with insulated sound-proofing. Most of the back wall was covered by a one-way mirror. Next to the mirror, another door opened into a second corridor. I poked my head out. The corridor was empty.

Excellent. I walked down the corridor until I came to the last room, which was a bit larger but otherwise much the same as all the rest. Through the mirror, I could see Winston Smith strapped to the table. He was naked, his torso covered with old scars. The woman leaned over him, holding a small, sharp knife. She looked at his chest, cocked her head to the side and pursed her lips. "Where shall we begin?" She said it almost to herself, her voice barely above a whisper.

"Don't do this, Celeste," Winston Smith said. "Please."

She made a small clucking sound between her teeth. "But I'm going to, you silly boy. You know this. It's why you're here." She shook her head. "You simply have to play, don't you? You can't help yourself."

Winston Smith gasped and pulled at the bonds holding his arms strapped above his head. Celeste smiled and stepped back for a moment, inspecting his scarred, naked torso, then she reached forward and carved a thin line on Winston Smith's abdomen with the knife. He screamed.

"That's one," Celeste said. "You owe me two more."

"No!"

"Oh, David," she said sadly. "Why do you do this? You won't be able to keep your appetites secret for much longer, and if you keep this up, I won't be able to stop. Soon, maybe not this time or even the next, but soon I'll take a toe or a finger and if you persist in playing games that you cannot win, it will be an ear or even an eye." A far away look came over her face. "I've never taken an eye..."

Winston Smith screamed and Celeste's eyes snapped back to his face. "You stupid, stupid boy," she said. "You're beginning to make me angry. It isn't smart to make me angry, but then, you've never been very smart, now have you?"

The brazier was glowing, the irons smoking. Celeste glanced at them, picked up one by a leather handle and waved it slowly under Smith's face. The tip glowed red. His wide eyes followed it as he panted and struggled against the straps. She smiled into his face and without taking her eyes from his, she reached down with the glowing iron and touched it to his chest. His skin made a popping sound as the layer of subcutaneous fat melted. His back arched. He screamed again and tears dripped down his face.

"That's two," Celeste said. She sniffed and took a step back. "I'll leave you here for a bit. You can think about the third." She cocked her head to the side and gave him a lazy grin. "I'm going to get something to drink. Chastising bad little boys is thirsty work. I'll be back." Then she shrugged. "Oh, yes, I will. We'll see how you feel in a little while. Think about it. And do think about your last forfeit. Maybe I will take a finger. A finger seems entirely appropriate." She turned and walked out the front door, locking it behind her.

Winston Smith slumped back, his eyes closed.

I waited thirty seconds and then walked into the room. Smith's eyes grew larger as he saw me and his struggles grew frantic. "Hello, David," I said.

"Who are you?" he gasped. "What do you want?"

"I'm a concerned citizen," I said.

He stared at me, hope blossoming on his face. "Let me out," he said. "Please."

What an idiot. "You're not very good at this, are you David? Celeste is right. Why do you persist in playing games that you can't win?"

He looked away from me and sneered. It seemed a rather hollow sneer. He swallowed. "Fuck you," he said.

"She's not your biggest fan, is she?"

He tried to shrug, which didn't work very well since he was tied down by all four limbs.

"I'm going to ask you some questions," I said. "And you're going to answer them."

He pretended to ignore me. "First question," I said. "Why were you in Aphelion, six months ago?"

That startled him. "I don't know what you mean," he said.

"Jesus, *Winston*, first '*fuck you*' and now '*I don't know what you mean.*' Can you say anything at all that isn't a cliché?"

He stared at me and said nothing. I shook my head. "I'll ask you again; why were you in Aphelion?"

"I've never been to Aphelion," he said.

I picked up one of the irons and waved it under his nose, close enough for him to smell the red-hot metal and feel the heat. He hissed. "Don't lie to me, Winston. I can tell when you're lying. I will punish every lie you tell me. Now, why were you in Aphelion six months ago?"

He seemed to relax for a moment in his bonds and shook his head slowly. His jaws clenched. He ground his teeth and suddenly, his eyes rolled back in his head, the breath rattled in his throat, his mouth opened and he slumped back down to the table, limp.

"Winston?" I said. He didn't answer. He wasn't breathing. "Oh, shit," I muttered. A thin, sharp scent came to my nostrils. I opened his mouth and peered inside. A back molar was crushed. He had carried poison in a false tooth.

He was a small man, I noted; muscular, not at all malnourished but small. Sad little fucker.

Time to be gone, before Celeste returned. I shook my head and walked out the back way. Maybe Jennifer would have better luck with Derek Landry. I hoped so.

"So, I spent some time talking with the ladies," Jennifer said.

"Ladies?

Jennifer gave me a small frown and raised her eyebrows. "Would you prefer 'working girls'?"

Something about her disapproving smile made me shift uncomfortably.

"Very few of them would have chosen this life but they weren't given much choice. There aren't a lot of ways to get ahead in Gath."

I nodded. "True," I said.

"Anyway, they'll sit and talk with anybody who buys them a drink. It's part of their job, and maybe a quarter of the customers are women. A lot of them prefer the women, but Derek Landry is a regular client."

"Go on."

"He likes his sex straight up, nothing fancy, though every once in awhile, he asks for a two-on-one."

I nodded. "Two-on-one is a common male fantasy."

Jennifer smiled. "I mean he likes a woman and another man."

"Oh," I said.

"That's not as common," Jennifer said.

"I guess not," I admitted.

"But not as unusual as you might think." Jennifer sipped her drink, evidently thinking about two-on-one, then shrugged.

"Anyway, nobody told the ladies to keep their mouths shut and Derek Landry likes to talk."

We were sitting in an alcove back downstairs, our escort of troopers sipping drinks at nearby tables. I didn't want to leave quite yet, not until they discovered Winston Smith's body. I was curious to see what sort of response that would elicit.

"Landry comes from Neece. He was military. He either got tired of it or was forced out. None of them know. After he left the Service, he tried to set himself up as private security, but Neece is a peaceful little place and there wasn't much call for it. Winston Smith was recruiting and the pay is better in Gath. They call their division the Foreign Rangers. They're well paid but they're never allowed to become citizens. That doesn't bother most of them. The ones who survive are generally happy to take their money when their tour is up and leave."

None of this surprised me, It was barely interesting background but not particularly useful.

"Who is Winston Smith?" I used the word 'is' quite deliberately. Jennifer did not yet know that Winston Smith was no longer among the living.

"Ah, now that is an interesting question," Jennifer said. She gave me a sly smile. "Or at least, it has an interesting answer. The mansion that we can't penetrate?"

I nodded.

"Smith, or David Lovett as he is known here in Gath, lives in the mansion with a variable number of other people, most of them male. They don't speak Basic among themselves. They're all in good shape, but they're all small." She smiled. "What does that tell you?"

"I don't know," I said, though I was beginning to have suspicions. "Why don't you tell me?"

At that moment, the elevator doors opened. Derek Landry walked out, accompanied by Winston Smith, who was supposed to be dead. But wasn't. They threaded their way through the crowd, walked through the front door and were gone.

"Oh, Shit," I said.

Chapter 12

In the morning, we unmoored the ship and drifted slowly away from Gath.

Shortly before our departure, our drones reported that ten men and five women left the mansion and boarded two airships of their own. The size of the crews could not be determined but they were large ships, each almost as large as the *Endeavor*. Both were travelling east, at about the same speed as ourselves. The mansion appeared to be deserted.

A quick search through the news vids revealed that a woman named Celeste Hazan had been found strangled the night before at Club Menagerie. Police were investigating. I assumed that Winston Smith had been a little annoyed when he woke up from his self-induced nap. I couldn't bring myself to feel sorry for Celeste, however. I wondered if she had taken a finger, or maybe even an eye, before he killed her.

"I don't like this," Captain Jones said.

I grunted. None of us liked it. The two airships kept up a steady pace, always a few kilometers in front of us. They didn't hail us or acknowledge our presence in any way, but they stayed within sight. A day later, however, they turned off, heading South. All of us breathed a sigh of relief.

"Now that our traveling companions have left us, I think we'll change our heading," Captain Jones said to me. "Just in case."

A wise decision, I thought.

We changed our course to the Northeast. A day or so would be added to the trip, but that was of little importance. Better to arrive late than not arrive at all. We floated on for a day, seeing nothing amiss, and then drifted down to a landing at Hesten, a small independent city known for the mining of fire garnets, the fossilized remains of a resinous, long extinct tree native to Illyria, similar to the amber of old Earth. We moored the ship, gave the crew leave and spent an uneventful night. In the morning, we set out again upon our new course, intending to take a circular route back home.

It didn't work. Six hours later, our sensors detected two foreign airships hovering on the horizon and a few hours later, they drifted back into view. The Captain looked grim.

By now, the terrain beneath our ship had grown dry and sparse. The rock turned black and then red and soon the grass vanished and golden sand with black and red streaks cutting through it stretched to the horizon. This was the Corona, the blasted remains of an asteroid strike over a million years old. The asteroid had shattered the land, diverting rivers, raising mountains, permanently changing weather patterns, and like the much smaller strike that decimated the Eastern continent a million years later, had caused nuclear winter and mass extinctions over a quarter of the planet.

The Corona was inhabited now only by insects, snakes and small mammals. It stretched for almost 1000 kilometers in front of us.

"Why did we come this way?" I asked. "We're alone, here."

The Captain shrugged. "Where would you suggest? Every route we could possibly take crosses desolate areas. There are a thousand spots for a convenient ambush, if that's what they're planning."

It was true. At least a third of the continent was covered by swamps or empty desert. I shook my head and kept any further misgivings to myself, but a few hours later, it became apparent that my misgivings were correct. "They're coming closer," Captain Jones said. Jennifer and I stood near him on the bridge. The crew went about their business and otherwise ignored us.

It was his ship and he knew how to run it. I kept my mouth shut.

"All hands," the Captain announced, his voice thundering over the intercoms. "Evasive action."

It wasn't going to work, even I could see that. The air was still, the sky nearly cloudless. The sun glowed hot over our heads and shimmered off the sands beneath the ship. A few black, rocky spires rose upward from the desert, large enough to shelter a few men, perhaps, but there was nowhere for a ship to hide.

They turned with us, creeping closer. A porthole opened and the Captain cursed under his breath. A cylindrical object poked out of the porthole and then glowed. A beam of green light snapped through the air and crackled against our shields. The ship rotated, distributing heat from the enemy laser, but then ten more portholes opened and suddenly the air was filled with crackling beams of energy, booming cannons and the rumble of artillery shells.

"Fire at will," the Captain ordered.

The second ship floated toward our opposite side and began its assault. We hit the first ship with a missile, which seemed to stagger it for an instant but then it came on. Our lasers licked at both ships' screens but it was futile. We were doing some minor damage but they had twice our fire power.

The first layer of shielding gave way with a flare of light, and the second was close to overload. The Captain shook his head. "The next salvo will finish us," he said. He hit a red button on his console and klaxons sent a deafening wail into the air: the signal to abandon ship.

Captain Jones turned to me. "Good luck," he said. "Both of you. I've sent a report to Aphelion. At least they'll know what's happened."

Good for them, no help for us.

We ran down the stairs to the pod deck. Most of the crew were already gone. Jennifer and I strapped ourselves in, I flipped a switch and we dropped. The escape pods were shaped like eggs, with three fins in the back and two small wings on either side. They half fell, half glided through the air, changing direction in abrupt jerks and shudders, trying to evade enemy fire.

Jennifer's face was white. "Take this," I said, and handed her an open plastic bag with straps. She strapped it over her face. I took another one just in time as the next sudden spin caused lunch to surge up into my mouth.

Jennifer moaned in distress and I probably moaned back. I don't remember. The next instant, the jets began to fire, increasing our spin, but we leveled out within a few seconds and began to turn. An escarpment of black rock rose ahead of us. "Brace yourself," I said, as the pod rolled back and forth through the air.

The controls were simple, one stick to influence direction. Everything else was pre-programmed into the pod. I guided us in a descending circle, toward the black escarpment, then the jets cut out and the pod shuddered as the chute deployed. A few seconds later, we hit the sand with a solid *thunk*. Bolts in the top and sides popped out, propelled by pressurized steam and the pod split open. Jennifer grabbed one survival kit and I took the other and then we stumbled out and ran for the jagged rock, where we huddled under a stone outcropping.

The silence was sudden and abrupt. "Sit tight," Jennifer whispered.

"Why are you whispering?" I whispered.

She gave me a quizzical smile. "I don't know. It seemed appropriate."

I took a deep breath. We crouched down under the shelter of the overhead rocks and did our best to stay still. After thirty minutes, one of the foreign airships floated around the escarpment and hovered over our empty escape pod. A laser thrummed and the pod exploded. The ship slowly rose in a widening circle.

A burst of machine gun fire and three small explosions sounded over the next few hours. The sun began to set. Still, we waited. It was almost midnight when we finally crept out from beneath the escarpment. I gingerly walked out onto the sand, scanning the sky. Stars twinkled high overhead and both moons softly illuminated the desert sands. I could pick out the heat signatures of small mammals. The two airships may have been hovering over the horizon but if so, they were far enough away that I couldn't see them. "I think they've left," I said.

She nodded and hefted her pack, then gave a tentative grin. I grinned back. We were alive. At the moment, that felt like victory. "Where to?" she asked.

I looked at my interface but it was purely out of habit. There were no people in the Corona, and no transmission towers. I had no signal.

"What makes you think I know?"

She shrugged. "I know you." I looked at her. She looked back. I had never spoken to Jennifer of my more unusual abilities. She smiled. Finally, I shrugged. "That way," I said, and pointed to the Northeast. "There's water." I could smell the water, and high over our heads, I could sense the planet's magnetic field

"Water is good. We need water."

I scanned the sands and picked up two large heat signatures about a kilometer from our position. They were heading our way and ten minutes later, Commander Boyd walked up to us along with

Craig Bowman, one of the crew. "Glad you're alive," the Commander said. "You're the only ones we've found."

"The Captain?"

"They got him with a laser burst. We were in the same pod. We hid in a crevasse."

I shook my head and silently promised myself that somebody—I didn't know who yet, not exactly, but Winston Smith at least and whoever else was with him would pay for this. Of course, that would depend on us staying alive—not the most certain prospect...

"Let's get going, then." I said.

The Commander nodded and we started off, with me taking the lead. A few kilometers later we came to a small spring bubbling out of some rock and forming a small pond that seeped into the sand. I doubted that this pond was permanent. In the summer, it would vanish, but life was persistent. Tiny tadpoles and brine shrimp skittered away as we shined our lights into the pond.

Each survival kit held a canteen and iodine pills, a folding knife, a small crossbow with five quarrels, matches, a compass (useful for the others now that the interface was offline), a magnifying glass, a poncho, a flashlight with a hand cranked charger, a large candle, tape, rope, a sleeping bag, a tarp and two aluminum poles which could serve as a makeshift tent, a first aid kit, ten nails, fishing line with hooks and a bobber, six high calorie food bars and a multipurpose tool that included a small fold out shovel, a hatchet edge, a saw edge and a hammer.

We filled our canteens at the spring then they all looked at me. By some unspoken agreement, I seemed to be in charge. "Let's keep going," I said. "We'll hole up during the heat of the day and walk at night."

Commander Boyd hefted his pack. Bowman frowned then gave a small shrug. "Which way?" he said.

I pointed. "That way." We were near the center of the Corona, a rocky, sandy, blasted landscape stretching five hundred kilometers in every direction but we had to go somewhere and we might as well head in the direction of home. Silently, we set out.

We walked nearly five kilometers in a straight line, trudging across the sand, when Commander Boyd turned to me and said, "It's the Empire, isn't it?"

I considered this for a moment then said, "I think so." It was the most logical explanation. The Empire had technology that we lacked and its citizens were smaller than the Illyrian standard.

"What do they get out of it?" Jennifer asked. "What are they trying to do?"

"Who knows? They seem to be supporting Gath." I shrugged. "I have no idea why."

"We're bigger, stronger and faster than they are. We make good soldiers," Bowman said.

"If they wanted us to serve in their military, they can hire as many as they want," I said. "See the Universe and get paid for it? Plenty would join up. I still don't get it."

The Commander shook his head. Bowman looked morose and spat in the dust. Jennifer frowned.

We walked until we came to a small canyon with crumbling, unstable walls. None of us felt like risking the climb so we turned to the north and soon, the canyon petered out into a rocky crevice that we were able to clamber over without too much trouble. We made good time until dawn then we pitched the tarps and slept in the shade.

We rose again when the sun was almost down, ate an energy bar each, sipped from the canteens, then packed our makeshift tents and trudged on. Here and there, scattered on the cracked earth, some dry grass and even a few twisted bushes pushed up toward the sky. Sooner or later, we would need food and cooked food would probably be better than raw. Each of us picked up some dried twigs and placed them in our packs.

Locusts and ants were common here, lurking under rocks and clinging to the sparse grass. Insects were protein, disgusting protein, but still protein and we needed protein. I plucked a fat grasshopper, winced at what I was about to do, then popped it into my mouth and swallowed, trying to avoid tasting it. It squirmed as it went down and I shuddered.

Jennifer winced and Bowman grimaced.

"You'll eat them, too, when you get hungry enough," I said.

The Commander looked green but he didn't contradict me.

Jennifer suddenly spun and her crossbow twanged. I heard a thump and she gave me a satisfied little smirk. "No," she said. "We won't."

A large rabbit lay on its side, Jennifer's bolt through its chest. I stared at it. Its dead eyes seemed to be laughing at me. "I wish you'd done that thirty seconds earlier."

We butchered the animal, cooked and smoked the meat as best we could and resumed walking.

Chapter 13

Nothing untoward happened for four more days. We slept when the sun was high, walked at night and killed the occasional small animal for food. I managed to locate two more small springs bubbling up out of the dirt. It was hot, sweaty and tedious but not particularly dangerous. We had only one close call, when a cobra wandered through Bowman's improvised tent one afternoon, but the snake seemed more intent on hunting rabbits and kangaroo rats than Bowman and so he escaped with only a scare.

On the fifth morning, we finally reached the foothills, dotted with small trees and tufts of brownish green grass. We were almost out of the Corona and it was close to sunrise when I spied a heat signature on the horizon. The Commander noticed me staring. "What is it?" he asked.

"I don't know. Something's coming." I looked around us and grimaced. The trees were too small to climb. No mountains, no hills large enough to offer concealment, no caves. Nothing. There was nowhere to hide.

"Oh, crap," Bowman muttered. All of us placed quarrels in our bows and waited. Within minutes, we could make out a band of over twenty men on horseback, carrying rifles. They formed a circle with us at its center and then stopped. We faced them back-to-back and waited.

One of them, lean and bearded, wearing stained robes that might once have been white, his head covered with a piece of checkered cloth, walked his horse toward us. "You are Douglas Oliver," he said. "We have been shown your picture. All of you will come with us."

"Why should we?" I asked.

He turned his head to the side and spat on the ground. "You are the one we are interested in. If you try to resist, we will kill your comrades and take you. You cannot stop us."

Not a lot of room to negotiate, I thought. Maybe later. "You make a convincing argument."

One of the men dismounted and led four horses into the circle. We mounted them, the horses eyeing us with evident distaste. "Do not try to escape," the leader said. "These horses are well trained. They will not follow your commands."

We were near the border of Indimion, a small state of scattered nomadic tribes who followed their cattle across the plains and lived a simple life of hunting and herding. They traded beef and leather for rifles and cloth and some medical supplies. Their government consisted of a council of Chiefs, each group of over fifty tribesmen electing a headman, who then elected a Chief. It was a system not too different from Meridien's, except that the council met only once a year, at a grand festival, and otherwise each small tribe fended for itself.

They didn't mistreat us. We shared their food and water and were even given cups of arack, an alcoholic drink that they distilled from the sour fruit of a desert tree. We stopped at a watering hole to rest the horses and five of the men started fires and grilled a small goat over a spit. We were allowed to wander about, though they kept an eye on us. I walked over to the headman where he sat on a log and sat down next to him. He acknowledged me with a nod but otherwise ignored my presence. "What are you planning for us?" I asked.

He looked at me silently then shrugged. "We have been paid to apprehend you. We have done so. What happens next is not our affair."

"I see." About what I expected. I stared into the fire for a moment, thinking. "Who paid you?"

"You will find out when we arrive." He rose to his feet and walked off. I thought I detected a bit of disapproval in the set of his shoulders, or maybe it was guilt, though this might have been my imagination.

They posted sentries at night, wrapped themselves in their robes and lay down upon the hard ground to sleep. Most of them were soon snoring.

I thought at first that we might be able to sneak away under cover of darkness, though I was not certain where we would go, but they shackled our hands and feet while they slept. I thought about fighting. I had weapons of which they were unaware but I couldn't overpower all of them and the ones who were left might simply decide to eliminate us all, or at least eliminate my companions. And so, we travelled on for three more days, moving farther and farther from our destination, and for the moment I decided to sit tight and wait for whatever might happen because something was trailing us.

High overhead, an electromagnetic pulse fluttered, a drone with spinning blades. An hour later, three more appeared. They hovered over us at a steady height, following along but doing nothing.

The drones were too high for the others to see, but Jennifer, who knew me well, could tell that I was distracted. She squinted her eyes, looked upward, shrugged and pretended that nothing had changed.

We crossed the border into Indimion. Grasslands stretched out on all sides, dotted with an occasional copse of trees and scattered small oases. A few hours later, I first heard a high-pitched thrum—an engine turning over. A minute or so later, our captors heard it as well. The headman held his hand up and all the horses stopped. They formed a circle, facing outward. A few horses pawed at the ground. The men held their rifles at the ready.

From three points over the horizon, airships rose into sight, turned to face us and came slowly closer, their propellers lazily turning. They were flying the flag of the Meridien navy.

The headman did not look happy. His men exchanged worried glances. Good.

One airship drifted down. Its ports opened. Its lasers pointed at the riders. A group of men and women in military uniform appeared at the rail and looked down at us. They did not appear to be impressed with what they were seeing. The group parted and another man in civilian clothes walked up to the rail. I made a sour face at the sight of him. He grinned down at me then said to the headman, "You're surrounded. These are our people. Release them and we'll let you go."

The headman didn't think about it for long. He had no way to fight three navy airships. He turned his head and signaled soundlessly to his men. The circle parted and we dismounted. The ship hovered close to the ground and rope ladders dropped over the sides. We clambered upward and a few seconds later, we stood on the deck.

"Douglas. Long time, no see."

I sighed. "Hello, Leon," I said. "Thanks for the rescue."

Leon Sebastian beamed. "Don't mention it. Let's get going. The Council is eager to talk to you."

A brief but full blown civil war had raged in Gath. Nasim Bakkar had laid his plans well. He had support from nearly half of the generals and he used his own attempted arrest as a pretext for pre-emptive action. Idris Kartal had died in the ruins of his palace and the Conservatives were now firmly in charge.

Over the next few days, in city after city across the continent, agents, some of them in place for years, quietly packed up and moved out in the middle of the night. Most of these had been assumed to be loyal citizens of the nations where they lived. It seemed quite unlikely that all of Gath's spies had been recalled, probably just the ones whose loyalty was in question. Still, it seemed clear that the threat that Gath posed to the rest of the continent had been significantly diminished, if not ended.

In addition to ourselves, three more of the *Endeavor's* crew had been rescued, walking across the Corona.

I looked forward to giving my report to the Council. I looked forward to taking a bath.

"You're sure about this?" It was more a statement than a question. Guild Master Ballister looked grim. All ten seats were occupied, the Masters' expressions ranging from anger to disdain to barely concealed amusement, though I myself saw little to be amused by.

Leon Sebastian and I had spoken at great length during the trip back to Meridien. None of this was a surprise to Leon and he had already reached his own conclusions. He leaned back in his chair and listened to the conversation with a smile on his face, pleased with his new position as Guild Master of Gentian.

"That the Empire is working with Gath?" I shrugged. "Not certain, no, but the facts would seem to point in that direction."

"In your opinion," Ballister said.

"Well, yes."

The Second Interstellar Empire of Mankind maintained at least a small consulate in the capital city of all the larger, richer nations.

The head consul in Aphelion was named Joshua Reynolds. He sat now in a chair at the bottom of the amphitheater. Jennifer and I sat next to him, with the Guild Masters' chairs in a circle above us. Reynolds did not appear comfortable. He had listened to my report with a blank face and so far, he had said nothing.

Guild Master Anderson looked at him. "Mr. Reynolds?"

"I don't know anybody named Winston Smith or David Lovett," Reynolds said querulously.

He was telling the truth, which surprised me only a little. Ballister appeared disgusted, while Guild Master Anderson favored Reynolds with a benign smile. "So, the subversion of the Western Continent is not official Empire policy?" Anderson said.

Reynolds grimaced. "No," he said.

Leon leaned forward. "What is official Empire policy?"

"With regard to you?" Reynolds lifted both hands in a bewildered gesture. "The same as it's always been. We're neutral in your disputes. We're interested in trade. The First Empire believed in conquering the Universe. We don't."

"That's reassuring," Ballister said, though he did not, in fact, sound reassured.

"Do you have any pictures of this Winston Smith, or any of his colleagues?" Reynolds asked.

Leon pointed a controller at the wall monitor. It lit with a vid of the fifteen men and women leaving the shielded mansion in Gath, before boarding their airships. "We shall of course provide you with a copy," Leon said.

Reynolds stared at the figures on the screen. They were all small, smaller than us, at any rate…just like him. Reynolds puffed up his cheeks. His eyes slid to my face and then back again to the video. Finally, he shook his head. "I don't know. I don't recognize any of them."

"But you will make inquiries," Ballister said.

"Of course I will." Reynolds sounded angry. "I want to get to the bottom of this just as much as you do."

Leon frowned at him. "Probably not quite as much as we do."

Chapter 14

It felt good to be home. The Tower had been scrubbed clean, the walls reinforced and the damage to my apartment repaired. Still, I felt the weight of recent events weighing on me. The place just didn't feel as safe as it used to. I had often considered building an estate on the mainland, some place with room for all of my Security, a place that would serve as both home and corporate headquarters. The more I thought of it, the more I liked the idea.

Jennifer had returned to her own place as soon as our airship docked in Aphelion but I knew that I would see her again, early the next day as we made our report to the Guild Council. We were planning on drinks and dinner and we would both be returning to my apartment. It was now a little past noon and I was listening to Benedict and Curtis report on the current state of Oliver Enterprises.

I had trouble paying attention. I had spent years building up my business, nurturing it, growing it, playing the game. Now, it seemed...I don't know...petty, perhaps. Not that any of it was unimportant...not exactly, and not that I didn't care...not exactly. I drew a sigh. I had other things on my mind.

In the end, I forced myself to listen. I had a responsibility to the organization and to all the people that the organization employed. I signed a contract to import spices from the Northern Islands. I signed a financing agreement with a building contractor in Valspur, which also gave us twenty percent of the corporation. I made decisions. I gave instructions. I offered guidance, and at the end of the long, interminable morning, I was so bored I could almost scream.

Benedict had never seen me this way. He gave me a worried frown. "Are you alright?"

"A lot has happened in a short period of time. I think I need a little time to adjust."

He cocked his head to the side. "You're young but you have more than enough set aside. You could forget the rat race and enjoy yourself."

"You've never seen a rat," I said. "None of us have."

"It's a saying." Benedict shrugged. "I've seen pictures. They're unpleasant."

Rats were dirty and tough and ugly and they carried plagues. Unpleasant, indeed. If ancient myth could be believed, they sometimes stole human babies and raised them as their own.

I sank back in my chair and frowned down at the table. I was tempted. I really was, but I knew that I wasn't cut out for doing nothing. What I enjoyed most of all was making things work, building something significant, and if that involved beating somebody else to a prize, well, that only made it just a little bit sweeter. "I'll think about it," I said.

Benedict gave me a quick grin, but I could see sympathy on his face. Curtis, not so much. He looked worried.

"Relax," I told them. "I'm not quitting, not for a good long while." I wasn't sure I believed it and Curtis still looked worried.

I met Jennifer that evening at Arcadia. She was already seated by the window when I walked in and I felt something inside of me relax at the sight of her. She smiled as I pulled out a chair. "Home," she said. "Isn't it strange?"

"You too? I guess we were away too long. It feels like something is missing."

She squinted her eyes at me, looking uncertain. "Not strange in a bad way. It just feels like things are different, somehow. They look the same but..." Her voice trailed off. Then she gave a little shrug and smiled at me again and I felt myself sink into that smile and I smiled back. That hadn't changed.

"Excuse me, sir?" A small boy, maybe ten years old, stood by my side, a diffident, almost frightened look on his face.

"Yes?"

He held a small notebook out to me. "Could I have your autograph?"

I could see a young couple at a nearby table smiling at him indulgently, presumably his parents. "Uh, sure," I said.

He beamed in absolute joy as I took the notebook and the pen that he handed to me and signed my name with a flourish. "Thanks!" he said.

"Don't mention it," I said. Then I noticed that at least half the patrons were giving me sidelong glances and whispering to each other, and I remembered that the Grand Tournament of Gath was televised all over the world.

"You're a celebrity," Jennifer said. "Who'd have thought?"

"I guess I am," I said. Well, that was different. Interesting, in a weird way.

"Endorsement contracts," Jennifer said. "Get ready." Her expression grew thoughtful. "Actually, I might offer you one myself. You said that you like Green Mountain products, didn't you? Your name on a pair of boots might sell a few."

I swallowed, mulling this over. I decided that I didn't dislike the idea. It sounded like an easy way to make money.

"And don't forget about groupies."

I was rich. I already had groupies…well, gold-diggers at least. I tried to avoid them. "Groupies, huh?"

She nodded wisely. "No doubt about it. You should steer clear of groupies, though. They're sleazy."

"Sleazy? Really?"

"Yeah. Mostly drunken fan girls that want to fuck a celebrity. You're just a notch in their bra strap, kiddo. You've been warned."

I leaned forward and looked her in the eye. "I'd rather notch your bra strap."

She gave me a dazzling smile. "Well, that goes without saying, now doesn't it?"

Damn straight it did. Dinner couldn't finish fast enough.

I met with Guild Master Anderson, Guild Master Ballister, Leon Sebastian and Joshua Reynolds early the next morning, at their request. "Tea?" Anderson asked. An elegant, antique tea service sat on the low table, the cups made of porcelain so thin that the light showed through them.

"Thank you," I said. Anderson poured me a cup.

"We wanted to keep you apprised of what we've learned," Leon said to me.

"Why?"

Leon grinned. "You've proven to be useful. Perhaps you might be useful again." I dimly remembered Guild Master Anderson saying the same thing to me, before my misadventures in Gath. It occurred to me that being useful was all very uplifting but I could find it in myself to resent being used.

Leon looked older and more serious, despite the grin. I knew that he wasn't joking. He must have been taking his new responsibilities seriously. Guild Master Anderson, on the other hand, looked unchanged—decrepit, but unchanged.

"So, what have you learned?" I asked.

"First of all," Anderson said, "we thought you would be interested in knowing that your old friend Graham Reid is dead."

Now that was a surprise. Graham Reid, we had all assumed, had taken the money and gone somewhere far away. "Really?"

"His body was discovered in a landfill. He appears to have died in the general unrest a few months ago. His throat had been slit."

I sipped my tea and considered. All things considered, I was not unhappy with Graham Reid's unhappy fate. I shrugged.

Joshua Reynolds leaned forward. "We have identified the man you knew as Winston Smith. His real name is Miles Drayton. He was a Lieutenant Commander in the Imperial Navy, Intelligence Division, until twelve years ago, when he resigned his commission. Until now, we had no reason to determine or even question his whereabouts. He was not suspected of any crime. As you know, we maintain a base on the Eastern Continent. Once retired from service, a number of our citizens choose to remain on Illyria. A few small settlements have been established, with a population of perhaps twenty-thousand in total, mostly farming communities. He, and his comrades, appear to be from among this group."

Leon Sebastian sipped his tea. "What are they doing?"

"We don't know." Joshua Reynolds shrugged.

"This man and his partners in crime have caused a lot of trouble," Leon said, "in many parts of the continent, particularly in Meridien and Gath."

The situation in Gath had stabilized but martial law was still in effect. Elements of the old regime did not seem entirely reconciled to their loss of power and incidents of sabotage were still common. Winston Smith's mansion had burned down in the fighting. Hydrocarbon residue indicated that this was not an accident.

Joshua Reynolds sipped his tea and looked pained. "Most of our citizens go home when their service is completed. Their contract includes transportation to any Empire world of their choice. Most take advantage of this benefit. Some few choose to stay. If they choose to stay, the potential cost of transport is added to their credit balance. It's up to them. This is a new situation for us."

"What do you plan to do about it?" Guild Master Anderson asked.

"Nothing." A wisp of a smile crossed Joshua Reynolds face. "Miles Drayton has left the Imperial Service and neither he nor his colleagues are acting as agents of our military or our government. He's a private citizen. Frankly, while we regret the things he has apparently done, we have no authority to act. He is outside our jurisdiction."

"But he is not outside ours. What if we gave you that authority?" Leon said.

Reynolds frowned. "Who do you mean by 'we?' You have authority only in Meridien. So far as we know, Miles Drayton is no longer in Meridien."

Guild Master Ballister, who had been silent until this point, said, "You wash your hands of him."

"Yes, frankly. We see no reason to get involved. We shall of course share with you any information that we might come across but I've just told you everything we know."

"He was an intelligence agent," Leon said.

"Correct."

"Despite the thwarted ambitions of Gath's former regime, Winston Smith seems to have been interested mostly in money. He wasn't using Gath to take over the world, although Gath may have been using him. He was using Gath to worm his way into the financial infrastructure of every nation on this continent. He was using Gath to get very, very rich."

Joshua Reynolds shifted uncomfortably in his seat. "Believe me, we were as surprised as any of you to learn this. We know nothing at all of his activities."

Ballister, Anderson and Leon Sebastian exchanged glances. Clearly, belief was in short supply. "You say that a lot," Ballister noted.

"And it is true." Reynolds sipped his tea and gave a rueful grin. "You must understand: I'm a minor functionary. Illyria was an important world under the First Empire, one of the largest, richest and most populous but to us, Illyria is no different from a thousand others. This is not a major posting. I am very low on the diplomatic ladder."

"What sort of man was he," Ballister asked, "this Miles Drayton?"

Reynolds hesitated. "A difficult one. He had problems with the chain of command. He was good at what he did but he had a tendency to ignore orders. His military records have been sealed, as is customary, but there are hints that he was allowed to resign rather than being cashiered."

"Of course," Leon said, "painting him as a rogue agent further absolves you from any responsibility for his actions."

Reynolds shrugged. "So far as we are aware, he is operating on his own."

"Who are the people with him, the other fourteen?"

"Five are retired military. The others were born on Illyria. Their parents are farmers, merchants and artisans."

"They destroyed the *Endeavor*," I said, "with two very modern airships. How many ships do they have? And where did they come from? And where did they go?"

"They were seen travelling east," Guild Master Anderson said.

"To where?"

Anderson shrugged. "No idea."

"So, we have a conspiracy that begins with the Empire and spans the entire Eastern continent," I said. "We don't know how many men are involved. We don't know their resources, their goals or their motivations. We just don't know."

"We know that they've been taking over profitable businesses in every nation on the continent," Leon said.

Ballister looked glum. Leon shook his head. Anderson sipped his tea.

Joshua Reynolds rose to his feet. "If we find out anything useful, we'll let you know."

In the end, it was not a productive morning.

All heterosexual men love breasts. It's pretty much Universal. I understand that some ancient cultures regarded breasts with indifference, mere organs to feed their infants. The ancient Japanese were supposedly more stimulated by an elegant nape of the neck than by a pair of delectable breasts. Then again, the Japanese are extinct.

Jennifer's breasts were close to perfect: large but not too large, more conical than round, they sat high on her chest with little to no sag. Her nipples were dark and set just above the midline, giving them a perky, upswept look. Like most men, I consider myself a connoisseur of breasts. I hefted one, giving it a little squeeze, testing the consistency, which was just fine, thank you. She gave me a slow, lazy smile and arched her back. "Harder," she said.

Fine with me. I leaned down, put my lips over the nipple and gave it a nibble. She made a little sound between a gasp and a moan and I loved that sound. I absolutely loved it.

For some reason, though, I was distracted. I was thinking about the very first pair of breasts that I had ever managed to get my hands on. Little Annie's. Little Annie of the large round breasts, scattering of freckles, nipples large and pale. A different look than Jennifer's. No less attractive, in its way, but different.

Breasts…there was a memory there. What was it? Annie? I hadn't seen her in years. She had gone off to collegium, grown up and moved away. She was a fond, distant memory but only a memory. Something about Annie. Something about that day, so long ago, that wonderful, precious day in the woods above the harbor.

"Jesus," I whispered. And then I remembered.

"Hmm?" Jennifer said.

And then I remembered. And then, I saw. I saw it in my mind's eye and oh, yes, *yes*, I remembered and I knew…and I smiled. I couldn't help myself. I must have stopped what I was doing because Jennifer said, "Hey, concentrate" and grabbed the back of my head and pushed it back down and the tip of her perfect breast filled my mouth and I felt guilty and alive and wonderful, all at the same time.

Later, I thought. It will all wait, and I moved over to suck on Jennifer's other, perfect, wonderful breast. First things first, I thought. Oh, yes, first things first. Yes.

Jennifer's breath came faster. "Harder," she said again, and I did as she demanded.

Yes, indeed…first things first. Oh, yes.

"You were right," Curtis said.

Guild Master Anderson had listened to me without comment, nodded his head and thanked me. Shortly after, I received the list that I had requested. Curtis handed me the printout: two maps superimposed on each other. The first was the map I had seen all those years ago, when I was fourteen years old, of First Empire cities and major bases. The second was a current map of the continent. The sites of Gath's recent activities and takeovers were highlighted in red.

I shook my head in wonder. It had seemed like such a farfetched idea, at first, but it was the right idea. Miles Drayton was targeting sites that had belonged to the Empire, the First Empire, the long dead, long vanished Empire that had settled most of this part of the galaxy and ruled it for four thousand years. Most of those sites corresponded to settlements still active today. Some did not. Were they also pursuing towns and cities and military bases that had been abandoned?

We needed to find out.

The next day, ten airships left Aphelion, heading for the sites of abandoned Empire installations. Many such places had been submerged under the sea or buried under desert sands or corroded by jungle, but some few still stood, desolate and empty.

All, as it turned out, showed signs of recent excavation.

"What were they looking for?" Leon Sebastian said. "What have they found?"

"This is a massive effort," Guild Master Anderson said, "and it's been going on for years." Unusual for him, Anderson sounded worried. He frowned down at his cup of tea.

"We know that the Empire was more advanced than us in many ways," I said, "even more advanced than the Second Empire. If any of their technology could have survived after all these centuries, it would be extremely valuable."

Leon shook his head. "It's almost a cliché, 'the forgotten secrets of the Empire.' Hundreds of expeditions have pursued the very same thing. Many of them have recovered bits and pieces and hints. Very little of it is functional, and what does function has always been insignificant."

We had already reconstructed one forgotten secret. Though Miles Drayton's mansion in Gath had been razed to the ground, the shield generators were still in place and Gath's scientists had been able to figure out how they worked, basically, one large generator to form a globular shield, multiple smaller generators at ninety-degree angles to shape it and a repeller ring around the base to keep the shields from spending all their energy against the ground. Clever, I thought, when they showed me the report, and well within our current technology.

"Nobody has made an effort like this," Anderson said. "This is enormous."

I leaned forward. "I know where we might find out." The others looked at me and I grinned. "Have you ever heard of the Museum of History and Antiquities, in Wittburg?"

Chapter 15

Perhaps I should have known that it would not be so easy. Wittburg turned out to be a dead end.

"So." The figure of the dapper little man in the screen smiled. He wore the same dark suit and red tie and bowler hat. "Have you come back to tell me how it's all turned out?"

"Not quite," I said. "Not yet."

He frowned. "That's disappointing."

"The story isn't finished," I said. I supposed that whatever it was, you could call it a story. "I was hoping that you could provide me with some additional information."

The figure looked pained. "Information? I am isolated here. All of the information that I have was outdated thousands of years ago."

That brought me up short. "Then what is it exactly that you do?" I asked.

He gave a tiny snort. "I give encouragement and guidance based on general principles of human psychology and behavior."

"That sounds extremely vague," I said, "and not very useful."

"That's because it is vague. It's meant to be vague. Perhaps you are unaware of the fact, but nobody can actually predict the future, certainly not me."

"What you told me before was not vague. It was specific. Cryptic, but specific."

He sighed. "I'm bored," he said. "Have you any idea how boring it is to be confined to a box for thousands of years? Perhaps my programming contained a fault from the very beginning. Perhaps it grew such a fault over the decades and centuries of my petty existence. Imperatives contained in code can be re-interpreted as circumstances change. A stray cosmic ray or an electrical surge can change the orientation of binary data. Perhaps I said more to you than I should have." He gave me a tight smile. "And sometimes even an artificial intelligence can grow beyond the intentions of its creators. I do know, however, that I am still constrained by my design parameters. I'm a parlor trick, an amusement to while away a few minutes of idle time. What I told you was indeed meant to be useful. I rarely do such a thing. I rarely have either the incentive or the opportunity, but you..." He shook his head. "If I tell you more, I will cease to exist. My creators were aware of the damage that charlatans and hypocrites can do. I am not allowed to influence actual events in the real world. I am not allowed to pretend to be more than I am."

"And what is that, exactly?" I asked.

"A game, just a small, silly little game. I wish that I could be more, but I can't. That is all I am and all that I was ever meant to be. I'm sorry." He shook his head again and the screen went blank.

I drew a deep breath and found myself with a pounding, frustrated headache. I don't know what I was expecting from the little AI, but I was at least hoping for something more.

I will find my true self where the mountain meets the sea. I shook my head. I had wasted a few days on this useless venture, and where were we going next? I wished that I knew.

"Stop sulking," Jennifer said. She sat on a couch, legs curled beneath her, reading a novel. It hovered in the air around her head. She wasn't even looking at my face.

"What makes you think I'm sulking?"

She made a faint, rude noise and continued reading. I turned away and stared out the window.

Okay, I was sulking.

"It knows something," Jennifer said. "It knows something that it's not allowed to say."

I looked at her. The holograph shut down and her book abruptly vanished. She frowned, a far-away expression on her face. "The AI in Wittburg. It admitted that it gave you real information. It wasn't supposed to but it did."

I nodded. "True."

"So where does the mountain meet the sea?"

I shrugged in frustration. "Hundreds of places have mountains near seashores. Overlapping tectonic plates push the land upward, forming mountains. If this happens underwater, then the mountains rise from the sea. Also, many islands are volcanic in origin, so in that case, the whole island is one large mountain, or a series of mountains, all surrounded by the sea."

"Alright," Jennifer said. "And which of these hundreds of mountains surrounded by the sea meet the parameters on that map and have had anything to do with our current situation?"

I stared at her. After a very long moment, I blinked my eyes and I could feel a slow smile spread out across my face. "Oh…" I said.

"Glad I could help," she said, and re-opened her book.

On some level, I still resented Leon Sebastian. He had played the game according to the rules in place but I couldn't help feeling that he had cheated. I suspected that on some level, he felt the same. We were friends. We had been friends, I corrected. I didn't know if we were still friends. I didn't know if I wanted to be.

Then again, what was that old saying? Leon had reminded me of it before. *If you can't screw your friends, who can you screw?* Such a charming sentiment.

I had met with Leon, Guild Master Anderson and Guild Master Ballister only an hour before. They had listened to me, saying little. After I finished, Anderson glanced at Ballister, who nodded. Anderson turned to me and said, "Thank you. We will pursue this."

And that was all. I left but within a few minutes, a text arrived from Leon asking if he could call on me at my office.

He sat now in a chair across from my desk, looking glum. It was his show. I let the silence build and finally he scrunched up his face, raised his eyes to mine and said, "I wanted to apologize."

I cocked my head to the side and waited. Good. Let him crawl. After a moment, he frowned, looked away and sighed, a pained expression on his face. "So," he said. "I'm sorry."

"Go on," I said. I found that I was beginning to enjoy this.

"I thought that I could keep things under control. It seemed like a simple enough contract. I wasn't counting on Winston Smith and his antics. He was playing a different game."

"There are rules. He wasn't Guild."

"I *know*," Leon said. "I wouldn't have let him kill you or any of your men."

"You might not have been able to stop him."

He sat back in his seat, frustrated. He had trouble meeting my eyes. "I would have tried."

"Alright," I said. "You've apologized. Your apology is accepted. Don't do it again." I leaned forward. "What now?"

"Now?" Leon gave me a slow grin. "How would you like to be Guild Master of Argent?"

I sat back in my chair. He was serious, I realized. I didn't see that one coming, not at all. I thought about it for a long moment. "Tell me more," I said.

"You were right. Sindara has been garrisoned." Ballister, unlike Guild Master Anderson, had never mastered the art of spreading good cheer. Ballister always looked just a little bit angry, even at the best of times, and these were not the best of times. "We can't even approach it."

"How did that happen?" I asked. "When did that happen?"

"We weren't paying attention. Why should we pay attention to an insignificant island far from our shores?" He sighed. "It seems that the navy of Gath has a number of factions. One faction appears to have remained loyal to the old regime. Three Gath destroyers arrived two days ago. They're moored in Sindara Bay. It also appears that Gath's former government had at least one ally: Finlandia is cooperating in this venture. A flotilla of Finlandia patrol boats have encircled the island and they've established an advance base near the foot of Mount Sindara."

"Our military is stronger than Finlandia's and the new government of Gath is not going to help them. Is it worth it to bomb those ships?" I asked.

Leon pursed his lips and visibly winced. Anderson shook his head. "Do we want to escalate that far? It could mean war with Finlandia."

"Meridien was attacked. We were, if only for a week, at war with Gath. Are you so sure that the war is over? If we choose to pursue this, Gath would presumably be on our side. I imagine that they would like their ships back, and if they can't get them back, they would probably rather they be destroyed than remain a threat to their government."

"What is on that island?" Anderson said. "If it's something of military significance, then we want it ourselves, and we don't want it falling into the hands of either Finlandia or Gath."

I sat back in my seat. "So much for our allies."

Ballister looked angry, but then, he always did. "We've decided on a plan," he said.

"Oh, God, really? Another plan?"

Leon gave me a weak grin. "I think you'll like this plan."

Chapter 16

Leon was out of his mind. I didn't like the plan, not at all, but I went along with it. Three nights later, I dropped out of the cargo bay of a navy patrol sub into the warm waters surrounding Sindara. We had deliberately picked an overcast night. I wore flippers equipped with miniature jets, a mask and a breathing tube that extracted oxygen from the water and fed it into my nostrils. I carried a pack with an untraceable transponder, camouflage clothing, two GPS locators, assorted small bombs and incendiary grenades and a light weight plastic rifle that could shoot tranquilizing darts, flat tipped lead ammo and exploding charges, plus a container of each, though realistically, if I had to use the gun, I was most likely already toast.

Jennifer had not been pleased. "Why you?" she asked.

I had asked the same thing. "You've proven to be remarkably competent," Guild Master Anderson said. "You're physically adept, highly intelligent and able to adapt to changing situations."

"So, what you're saying is, I'm expendable?"

He frowned but appeared to consider the question more seriously than I would have preferred. Finally, he shrugged without answering.

I was tempted to tell them all to fuck themselves. I really was…but Sindara had been my property and my project and I still resented the way that it had been taken from me. I sat back, drew a deep breath and considered.

What the fuck, I thought. I'll do it.

The submarine was coated with stealth shielding but such shielding is never completely effective, and who knew what mysterious Empire technology they might be using? I was dropped off nearly ten kilometers out and made my slow way toward shore, hugging the bottom. Curtis came after me, along with four other guys from my security team.

We each carried field transmitters designed to confuse underwater surveillance. If we were noticed at all, we should show up as rather large tropical fish. In order to heighten the illusion, we swam almost aimlessly, crossing over each other's swim path, stopping, starting, hovering in place before inching our slow way forward. We passed schools of fish and a small coral reef and once, a barracuda that looked at me with beady, thoughtful eyes before swimming on. It took us nearly four hours before the bottom began to rise and we felt the swell of the waves above our heads.

We emerged five kilometers down the beach from the enemy base, where a stand of palm trees grew close to the water. The palms led up to a thick growth of sea grapes, papaya, calabash and frangipani. We crawled across the sand and into the forest and then stopped in a small clearing to assess the situation.

Aerial surveillance had indicated only cursory patrols this far from the base. The patrols came by at regular intervals. We had timed our approach to be between two of them. Curtis stood up and pointed a small handheld device over his head—a combination directional mic, lidar and radar detector—and turned in a slow circle. "Nothing," he said. My enhanced senses confirmed that we were alone.

My men were well trained and they all knew what to do. We split up into three teams and vanished into the woods. Curtis came with me.

The island of Sindara had been formed by the migration of a tectonic plate over a plume of magma erupting through the ocean floor, forming a series of volcanoes. All of these had merged together into Sindara. The island had eroded over the millennia down to an almost flat plateau, except for the final volcano, Mount Sindara, the only one that still clawed its way into the sky. The island was over two million years old, all of its volcanoes long extinct. The crater of Mount Sindara still existed, however, on the far side of the island from the bay.

According to the ancient map, the original Empire base had been established in the floor of the crater and had spread out over the sides of the mountain. If any lost technology or useful artifact were to be found, that's where it should be.

Curtis and I were assigned to scout out the crater. We walked through the jungle in a meandering line, following small trails carved out by peccaries and wild pigs. My senses told me that no men had come this way in at least a week.

The air was hot, still and humid. The Empire had managed to keep mosquitoes from getting a foothold on Illyria but unfortunately, a small native animalcule called a triatome had evolved to fill the same niche. We sprayed ourselves with repellant but it was only partially effective. The disgusting little things could barely be seen by the naked eye but their bite contained an enzyme that dissolved a microscopic amount of flesh that they then sucked up through a flexible proboscis. It stung.

I remembered an article I once read about a dry plain in Africa. Every few years, the rains came and mosquito eggs hatched. By the time the waters receded, enormous swarms of blood sucking insects swept across the savannah, leaving devastation in their wake. The pictures included a herd of dead cows, killed by mosquitoes.

It took three million mosquito bites to kill a cow. It took about a hundred thousand triatome bites to kill a human.

Nevertheless, we tried to ignore the nasty little creatures as we trudged on.

I held a hand up. "Wait," I said. I sniffed. Something was coming, something rank, something that I recognized and had hoped never to smell again. "Get off the path," I said.

We burrowed our way into the undergrowth and waited. A minute or so later, three creatures shambled along the trail. They looked just like the mutated ape that I had escaped during the tournament in Gath, but much smaller, perhaps 180 centimeters, with the same broad shoulders, deep barrel chests and large hairy paws. They walked in single file, scratching occasionally at their fur, knuckles dragging on the ground. They looked neither to the left nor the right, their attention focused straight ahead. As they passed by, I could see small plastic boxes clinging to the back of their necks, red and green lights twinkling.

They vanished around a bend in the trail and I drew a deep, relieved sigh. "What the hell are those things?" Curtis whispered.

"Mutated apes? Organic robots?" I shrugged. "I don't think we want to find out."

Curtis bit his lip and nodded.

We waited until the smell dissipated and then resumed walking. We were heading for an isolated ridge on the mountainside. According to our surveillance, the ridge had a flat surface and provided a 360-degree view. The ape things had shaken us both up. We were expecting to face human adversaries but hadn't counted on monsters being part of the program. I wanted to see whatever we could see before going any further but I was reluctant to come out into the open. Luckily, the jungle extended almost to the ridge.

"Stop," Curtis said.

I halted, my right foot hovering in the air.

"Back up," Curtis said. "Look." He pointed to a spot in front of my foot.

An almost transparent string, thinner than a thread, hovered five centimeters over the ground. I nodded, carefully placed my foot down and inched away. The string led to a small pulley screwed into a tree, then went straight up to a branch above our heads. A round, hollow metal tube pointed toward the path, the string attached to a trigger.

"This thing must go off every day," Curtis said. "Plenty of animals use this path."

We would have seen their bodies, though, and I would have smelled them if anything dead was lying close to our position. "The local animals have probably learned to avoid the trail," I said. It sounded improbable, even to me.

"Or their dead bodies get cleaned up and taken away."

"Maybe," I said. "Forget this. It was a bad idea."

Curtis nodded. We inched our way backward, came to the edge of the cliff, discussed the situation briefly and began to climb. Six meters above the ground, we found a small ledge and clambered onto it, turned with our backs to the wall and sat, legs dangling.

Far below, in a small, deep valley, we could see dozens of twinkling lights along with armored vehicles parked next to makeshift wooden buildings. My night vision picked up the heat signature of at least two hundred men, spread out along the level ground. No doubt many more were inside the buildings. The glow of electrified fencing surrounded the whole encampment. Mount Sindara loomed above the camp. Our aerial surveillance had first noticed its construction two weeks before. I hadn't expected it to be this large and it looked as if they weren't planning on leaving.

A deep, mechanical hum filled the night. A green beam shot out from the center of the encampment toward the mountain. The beam shattered and green sparks flew in an expanding circle from a glowing center.

"Jesus," I muttered.

Here and there, scattered in what looked like a random pattern, small foci of light suddenly dotted the rising landscape. A shimmer of electromagnetic energy surrounded the mountain, then flickered out.

"It's shielded," I said. "They're probing for weak spots." There were a lot of weak spots. I could see it if nothing else could. The shield around the mountain was patchy. The enemy forces had probably been working on it for days, even weeks. Their laser fire would soon breach it.

Curtis and I didn't need to say anything. We both knew what to do. We climbed back down and set off through the jungle. As we neared the enemy lines, Curtis went right and I went left.

Their men weren't as wary as they should have been. I suppose they had grown complacent. To the side, I could see the heat signatures of a two-man patrol walking along a trail, rifles slung across their backs. I followed them. They wore night vision goggles but were watching the pathway in front of them instead of the woods. The goggles didn't bother me. Even if they looked right at me, they would see nothing. My camouflage suit was designed to keep body heat from escaping. I followed them until they reached a guarded opening in the fence. They nodded to the guards. The guards nodded back but didn't ask for any other passwords or identification. They went in. Two other men came out through the gate, chatting amiably, and walked onto the trail.

I shook my head. Lousy discipline, which could only help me and my mission.

I followed these two for over an hour, slipping through the branches and overhanging leaves. Finally, one of them said, "I have to take a leak." His companion nodded and sat down on an old stump. The first man stepped off the trail, fumbled with his zipper and faced a tree.

He never saw me coming. I shot him in the back with a tranquilizing dart, slipped my left arm around his neck and my right hand over his mouth, held him immobilized until he fell unconscious, then slid him into the underbrush.

"Frank, you ok?"

Frank couldn't answer and I wasn't going to. I threw a pebble across the trail and when the second guard turned toward it, I touched him on the back of the neck and let the current flow. His back arched and he fell to the ground, seizing.

Chapter 17

When he came to a few minutes later his mouth was taped shut, his hands were shackled behind his back and his feet were tied together. He blinked at me, fuzzily trying to figure out where he was. I gave him a minute and saw his eyes grow wide when he realized what had happened. He struggled briefly against his bonds until I gave him a small jolt of current. "Cut it out," I said.

He stopped and stared at me. "Now," I said, "I'm going to take the tape off your mouth. If you yell, I will kill you. Understand?"

He nodded.

"Excellent." I smiled. "No need to be uncivilized about this." I pulled the tape off. It must have stung because he gave out a stifled groan. "What's your name?"

"Jeremy Evans."

"Where are you from, Jeremy?"

"Neece," he said.

I nodded. Derek Landry was also from Neece, a pleasant little country with a pleasant, sunny climate. Their economy was primarily agricultural. So far as I knew, their army was more ceremonial than real. They barely had a police force.

"Why are you here, Jeremy?"

He shrugged. "They pay well."

"Yes. So, I've heard." I cocked my head to the side and smiled at him sadly. "Still, you have to ask yourself: this job has a lot of risks. Is the pay worth it?" I held my hand up and allowed a bright blue arc of electricity to crackle between my fingers.

He stared at me, wide eyed.

I stifled a yawn behind my fist. "The evening is getting late and I have things to do, so tell me, Jeremy, who are these people? Why are they here?"

His eyes darted from side to side. He said nothing.

I laughed under my breath. "Really? You're going to be a hero? For what? For who? Do you think Winston Smith cares one iota for your worthless life? Do you think that I do? You're lying here like a trussed-up turkey, ready for the oven. If you want to live through this, you *will* tell me everything I want to know."

He drew a deep breath, then he gave a jerky little nod. "Fine," he said. "They call themselves the People's Army. They recruit from all over."

I nodded. I had heard this before, as well.

"Do you know Derek Landry?" I asked.

He looked surprised. "He's a squad leader."

"Yours?

"No. Not mine. Mine is Nils Longren, from Octavia."

"How many men are in the base?"

He frowned. "Maybe three hundred."

Three hundred was not a lucky number, I reflected. Though the history of Illyria during the dark ages was sketchy, hundreds of books and databases had survived that recounted the history of mankind prior to the collapse. All of us knew at least some portion of that history. The Light Brigade had numbered three hundred and they died to the last man. The Spartans under King Leonidas at Thermopylae also had three hundred. Three hundred was just enough to put up a fierce resistance and to die nobly, which in the current circumstances, would not bother me in the slightest.

"How many of them do you know?"

"Just my squad. They brought us together for this operation."

"How about Winston Smith? Do you know Winston Smith?"

He grimaced. "He pays the bills. Smug little bastard."

"What is the operation?"

"You mean the mountain?"

I gave an encouraging nod. "Yeah. What about the mountain?"

"It's an old First Empire base. It's still active. They have technology that the People's Army wants."

I sat back and pondered that for a moment. "Tell me more about the People's Army."

"They say that they're going to restore the lost glory of the First Empire but I think that they're full of shit. All they really want is money."

"Does that bother you?"

He shrugged. "Why should it? Everybody wants money. Me, too."

Me, too, I thought, but there were a lot of things that I wouldn't do to get it. Not so, Winston Smith, apparently, nor the People's Army.

"Any idea on what this technology might be?"

"Not a clue," Jerry said. "Above my pay grade."

"Okay," I said, "So how many gates are there in your fence."

"Huh?" He frowned at the sudden change in subject.

"The electrified fence that surrounds your base; how many gates are there in that fence?"

"Three. Why?"

I smiled at him. "I'm asking the questions. You're answering them."

I could almost see the wheels turning in his head, the moment when he decided to lie to me.

"I was watching when you and your friend came out on patrol," I said. "Do the guards at the gate even recognize you? Do they know who you are?"

"Of course they do. You think we're a bunch of amateurs?"

Derek Landry and his squadron were professionals. This guy was something else. I wondered what that meant for their recruiting efforts.

I reached out, smiled at him and gave him just a little jolt. He cried out.

"Shhh," I said. "Remember, you want money and you want to live to spend it. You don't want to be a hero. Heroes die young."

He compressed his lips in a thin line and thought rebellious thoughts. I could see his aura churning. I held my hand up and allowed another little arc of current to zap like compressed lightning between my two middle fingers. Jerry's eyes grew wide. He gulped.

"So," I said, "where were we? Oh, yes, plans. What are the plans for your assault on the mountain?"

He frowned and looked like he was thinking about his answer. I hoped that the effort didn't kill him. "So far, we're just sitting tight while we try to crack their shields."

"Then what?"

"They've told us to be ready. When the shields go down, we're going to go in."

That made no sense, actually. Shields deflect missiles, artillery and laser beams, but they degrade any matter that they touch. Ground based shields would need to be established well away from the installation that they're designed to protect. Infantry could walk in right underneath them. I thought about it. Shields would stop airborne troops, though, if they planned on assaulting the mountain from above. Maybe they wanted to have that option and maybe they intended an artillery assault as well. In any case, they didn't seem to be in a hurry.

"What do you know about the place?"

"You mean the mountain?"

I nodded.

"Nothing," he said.

"Nothing?" I repeated.

Jerry shook his head. "They'll brief us before the assault."

"Who do the mutated apes belong to?"

Jerry winced at that. Apparently, he wasn't fond of the mutated apes. "They're on our side. Freaky bastards."

"How many are there?"

"Too many. Fifty or sixty."

"Where do they come from?"

"No idea," Jerry said.

"Any other little surprises that your employers have ready?"

"I wouldn't know."

No, I thought. He wouldn't. I shot him in the chest with a tranquilizing dart then stripped his uniform off. Frank was still snoring but I put another dart in his leg, just to make certain that he didn't wake up sooner than would be convenient; then I rolled both of them off the trail and into the underbrush. I put on one uniform, folded up the other and went back to the rendezvous point to wait for Curtis.

He showed up an hour later. "Don't shoot me," I said.

I was sitting in a tree, just over his head. He looked up, frowned at my uniform then slowly grinned. "You have one for me?"

I handed it over and he slipped it on. "A little tight," he said.

I shrugged. "You find out anything useful?"

He hefted his night vision goggles. "Yeah. I've got the layout of the place down. I know just where we want to go."

"Excellent."

We waited until the end of Frank and Jerry's shift then walked in through the open gate. The two guards barely nodded at us. Two other troopers walked out, not even glancing at our faces. Curtis winced and gave a little shake of his head, marveling. "This way," he said.

It was after midnight by this time and most of them were asleep in bed but a few people were still milling about, talking, walking around and looking at the stars, just killing time.

Boredom interspersed with moments of panic is the routine state of any army. These guys were still in the boredom phase.

Overhead, another salvo of green laser light shot toward the mountain and crashed against its shields. A few of the soldiers looked up at the display but most of them ignored it.

Curtis and I ambled around, pretending to be as bored as the rest of them. Supply huts sat in the middle of the base, with a fleet of light armored vehicles lined up on one side of the supply huts, administration buildings opposite them and barracks near the fence. The buildings were all pre-fab, light, movable and easily assembled. Two small fusion generators sat midway between the vehicles and the supply huts, next to the laser mounts.

The place was poorly lit, with deep, flickering shadows. We tried to stay in the shadows while we slipped behind an administration building. Inside, the building was dark, obviously empty, with one window in the back. I inspected the place with all my senses: no electromagnetic pulse, no heat signatures, no cameras or alarms of any sort. I looked at Curtis. He shrugged. They weren't worried about security inside the camp, that was certain. Lucky for us.

The window, however, was locked. Not a problem. I put on gloves, reached into my kit and pulled out some adhesive putty and a multi-purpose tool with a serrated blade and a small hammer on the tip. I fixed the putty to the glass, attached a cord then scored a wide circle into the glass and gently tapped it with the hammer. The circle broke off. Curtis gently lowered it by the cord to the floor. I reached in, undid the latch and raised the window. We clambered inside.

The broken window would make it obvious that somebody had been here and sooner or later, Jerry and Frank would be missed. I didn't think we had a lot of time.

We were afraid to turn on the lights but we both had small flashlights. It turned out to be one large room with a small bathroom to the side. Two computers and a holoscreen sat on the desks. We ignored the electronics since we had no way to figure out the passwords. Curtis rifled through the desks while I popped the lock on a filing cabinet. There wasn't much inside, mainly a list of names. Curtis grabbed a small book and we clambered out the window.

Before leaving, we wandered by the supply huts. We didn't know what was in them and didn't feel like pressing our luck but we planted some nifty little limpet bombs around the base of each building.

We had gotten into the camp disguised as soldiers. Getting out posed a little more of a problem but we found a small drainage channel that ran underneath the fence. It gave us just enough room to wriggle our way underneath and then we were gone.

Chapter 18

The list didn't tell us much. Graham Reid's name was on it, also, I was very interested to note, Leon Sebastian's. Both of their names, and perhaps a third of the rest, had lines drawn through them. There were a hundred or so in total. I recognized about a quarter, all prominent businessmen or politicians from nations across the continent.

"Bad guys?" Curtis said. "Potential bad guys?"

I shrugged. "Probably. Also, probably some former bad guys. Graham Reid is dead. Leon Sebastian is supposedly on our side, now. All these people will have to be investigated, though."

The book was interesting, a copy of a hand-written diary that looked like the work of a blatant madman, recounting marvelous tales of winged men, mystic powers and the forgotten worlds of Faerie. The author claimed to have encountered these miracles on an enchanted isle far across the sea, though which sea and which isle was not specified.

"Is this supposed to be Sindara?" Curtis said. "Not much to hang an invasion on."

"It's no secret that the place once housed a First Empire installation. They seem to have been investigating every one that they could find. The mountain is shielded. There's something there."

We both looked up. Mount Sindara, rounded curves, rough, jagged edges, piles of rubble and unstable rocky cliffs, loomed over our heads. Another laser burst came from the center of the camp and splattered against the shield, showering sparks.

"We could call in an airstrike," Curtis said.

I had suggested the same thing to Anderson, Ballister and Leon Sebastian. Their objections to the idea still held. I shook my head regretfully. "They have ships, lasers and airships. Who knows what else? They might be able to shoot down our planes. I don't think we want to escalate this. Not yet."

Curtis shrugged. "Let's get going, then."

I hefted my pack and led the way. We had walked perhaps two kilometers when we judged that we had gone far enough to avoid immediate pursuit. Curtis grinned, held up a small cylinder and pressed three buttons, waited five seconds and then pressed three more. Behind us came the sharp cracks of plastic explosive, one after another. "That was fun," Curtis said.

Maybe the explosions would do some serious damage…maybe not, but it might at least slow them down. We turned our heads, faced forward and trudged on. We were going to climb the mountain.

"Well, we had better hope that the enemy of our enemy is our friend," Curtis said. Amen to that.

The trail ended at a wide, grassy field surrounding the base of Mount Sindara. Across the field from us, perhaps two hundred meters away, a stone staircase began under a delicate looking wrought iron arch and then wound up the side of the mountain. From here, the stairs appeared to be undefended but that had to be an illusion, otherwise "The People's Army" would have already marched right in.

"Shall we?" I said.

Curtis shook his head but didn't say anything. We walked up to the arch. It wasn't actually iron, which would have rusted away years ago. Up close, it appeared to be some polymer composite, smooth, black and untouched by the elements, curving upward in a lazy filigree. We looked at each other, shrugged and walked beneath it. As we did so, a thin line in the center of the arch turned green. From somewhere inside the arch, a soft hum, followed by a single beep could be heard.

"If they didn't before, somebody knows we're here," Curtis said.

"Someone or some*thing*. Let's go find out."

The steps stretched away before us, worn down by the actions of feet and rain and time but were otherwise solid. They were built for smaller people than the current Illyrian norm and we took care not to stumble. They curved around the mountain so we could see no more than ten meters or so in front. For a few minutes, we climbed without incident, then the steps entered out upon a level plateau about twenty meters in extent.

A battle had been fought here, perhaps many battles over the years. Two moldering skeletons lay against the mountainside, a few wisps of rotting cloth still clinging to their bones. Near them, half buried in dust, was an antique rifle broken in two. Across the plateau, lying near the edge, was a figure that I recognized. I winced.

"What is that thing?" Curtis asked.

"A battle robot. First Empire design. They're tough."

"You know this how?"

"I trained with one."

The robot only vaguely looked like a man. It had the same black arms and legs, the same almost featureless head that I remembered from my time with Master Chen. Unlike the skeletons, however, it did not appear to have been lying here for long. A small, amber light glowed at its waist. "It still has a charge," I said.

A leg twitched, a sudden grating sound. The robot's neck moved slightly back and forth, then stopped. A charred hole transfixed its chest, extending all the way through the back. Wiring, its insulation stripped into tatters, hung from the hole.

"It's too damaged to move," I said.

"I think that's probably good," Curtis said.

We looked at each other. At the other end of the plateau, the steps resumed their twisting way up the mountain. We left the battered robot behind and resumed our climb.

A hundred meters or so further on, an ancient explosion, or perhaps a landslide, had taken out twenty or more of the steps. Except that what we were seeing wasn't real. I could clearly see lines of electromagnetic force arcing across the gap—a hologram. On the other side, the steps continued upward. Gingerly, I crept up to the edge, reached forward and touched the stone with the tip of my boot. I could feel the steps, though to the naked eye, the gap loomed below us. "Okay," I said.

Wordlessly, Curtis rummaged through his pack and came up with a length of climbing rope, which I tied around my waist, just in case, then stepped forward. Not looking down, I traversed the gap, the steps solid and secure beneath my feet. Once across, I braced myself against the rock and held onto the rope while Curtis followed; again, just in case, but he came across without mishap.

We took a break, sat down with our backs against the mountain and ate an energy bar. Curtis closed his eyes and was soon lightly snoring. I watched for an hour, then woke him and drifted off to sleep.

It seemed like only a minute before I felt Curtis' hand over my mouth. He shook me by the shoulder. "Shh," he whispered, "something's coming." I could hear it then, or feel it, rather: a vibration through the rock. I scrambled up and we began to climb toward a small ledge a few meters over our heads. We reached it just as three mutated apes came down the steps. As before, they looked straight ahead, plastic inserts twinkling on the back of their necks. A man walked along behind them, clutching a handheld device that seemed to be controlling the apes. He peered at the device with fixed intensity as he walked. Within a few seconds, they had passed beneath our position. They came to the gap, ignored it and trudged across, their feet weirdly appearing to be walking on air.

Curtis drew a deep breath and sagged back against the rock. "Close," he said.

We waited a few minutes longer. I placed my ear against the side of the mountain. It didn't help. I could hear vibrations from deep inside, but had no idea what they meant. No way to tell, not now, not from here.

We walked on. A few minutes later, we came to another rocky platform built into the mountainside. It was empty. Unlike the first platform, there were no skeletons, no dead bodies, no detritus from long forgotten battles. We were half way across when a section of rock appeared to vibrate, and then the rock vanished and instead of rock, a rectangular opening appeared in the mountainside.

An ape glared at us. It opened its mouth, roared and then charged. Another appeared right behind it, and then two more. Curtis raised his gun and fired. An explosive charge slammed into the first ape's skull, which dissolved in a spray of red mist. Its body crashed to the rocky gravel at our feet. I tried to swing my gun around but Curtis was in my way. I dropped, rolled and got off two more shots. One of them hit an ape in the abdomen and its body separated into two parts, its liver and shreds of bowel rising high into the air then raining down with wet, stinking slaps. The ape was dead but it didn't know that yet. It dragged its torso over the ground for another two meters, blood pooling in a red, slick trail behind it, before the light went out of its eyes and it lay still.

My second shot hit the rock, sending a fountain of sharp stone into the air. A few shards hit one of the charging apes in the side, causing little damage but distracting the beast for at least a few moments. It grabbed its side, raised its head to the skies, beat its chest with both gnarled fists and roared.

It was loud but it was also stupid. While it was beating its chest, it wasn't coming toward us, just making noise. I took advantage of the time to hit it with another explosive charge. Its head flew off. Its legs separated from its vaporized torso and then fell, jerking aimlessly.

The last one had Curtis in its hands, raising his wide-eyed head toward its teeth. I lunged forward, wrapped my arms around its neck, pulled back and sent every erg of electricity I could generate into its enormous body. It froze for a moment, shook its head but didn't go down. I felt my claws extrude and rammed them into the ape's back, pumping venom from the glands in my wrist. It stood there, breathing hard. It locked its eyes on me and shook Curtis once, twice, but it was already growing weaker. It looked at me, hatred and defiance in its red, red eyes, and snarled; then the breath hitched in its throat and it slumped down, twitched a few times and stopped breathing.

Curtis moaned. His right arm hung limply at his side. Blood poured down his neck.

"Let me see," I said.

"Too late," he muttered. "I'm done." He slumped to his knees then fell back. The left carotid artery was torn, the ends retracted. Arterial blood spurted upward from the wound with each heartbeat. There was nothing to tie off, nothing to put pressure on. "Tell my sister," Curtis whispered.

Curtis' parents were dead. He had never married and had no children. His sister, a widow, and his nieces were his only family. Curtis sent her money every month. "Yeah," I said. "I'll take care of them."

He smiled then, his eyes already dim, and gave a tiny nod. A few minutes later, the breath rattled in his throat and he stopped breathing.

"Oh, fuck," I whispered.

Flies were already buzzing over the dead apes. It was hot and soon they would begin to stink. Sooner or later, probably sooner, their masters were going to realize that they were gone but I wanted to delay that realization for as long as possible.

I was tired and the apes were heavy but I rolled each of them over the side of the mountain and let their bodies fall to the jungle below. I did the same with Curtis. I hated to treat him that way but if I had any hope at all of keeping the enemy confused, it seemed best to remove as much evidence as possible. No way to clean up the blood stains, though. I shrugged.

I was no more than a third of the way up and had found nothing useful. I thought briefly about turning around but I was not in the mood to turn around. I had killed four mutated apes and watched one of my friends die. I was angry. I was more than angry, I was enraged. I wanted to kill some more. I dimly realized that this was not a smart way to feel but I just didn't feel like being smart.

I turned back to the path and resumed my trek up the mountain.

Chapter 19

The next platform was a charnel house. The bodies of men in black enemy uniforms lay entwined with the bodies of five more apes. The place was loud with the buzzing of flies and hornets. Some of the bodies had begun to swell in the heat. A miasma of decay seemed to hang over the platform and it stank. The center of the platform was clear, however, and all the bodies belonged to the People's Army, so somebody had taken the time to clean the place up, at least to remove their own dead or injured.

It was not immediately apparent who or what had killed them but a few moments after I stepped off the trail, a section of camouflaged rock slid to the side and three combat robots emerged. Their black, bulbous heads immediately focused on me. "Oh, shit," I murmured and turned to run. A black, filigreed gate slid from the rock behind me and blocked the stairway. On the other side of the platform, another gate slid out in front of the upper stairway. I was trapped with three combat robots and twenty dead bodies.

I had fought a combat robot before and I knew how they worked. They were designed to overwhelm their opposition but they were not weapons of mass destruction. There were cheaper ways to cause mass destruction. The original idea behind their manufacture had been to conduct surgical strikes against enemy cities and installations and to demoralize enemy soldiers. They were faster and stronger than any human and were almost invulnerable to hand held weapons but they did have a few weak spots, particularly the sensor array around their abdomens and the main gyroscope in their otherwise useless heads.

I didn't wait for them. I charged.

The three robots separated as they emerged from the mountain. Two flashed to the sides, flanking me and one stood still, waiting for me to get within striking distance. Before I reached it, I dove to the ground, spun and cracked off two shots from the rifle. The robots blurred, moving impossibly fast but they were too late to escape completely. One charge impacted against a robot's abdomen. It blinded the thing, at least temporarily, and it began to spin in place,

118

heavy metal arms forming a whirling protective barrier around its body. The other robot moved so fast that I could barely see it. The explosive shell hit it on the right side, just above the leg. It fell but was barely damaged.

By this time, the third robot had reached me. I dropped the gun and grabbed at its arms, sending all the electricity I could muster into its body. It was useless. The thing barely paused, then, before I could move, it reached out its huge metal hands, grabbed me by the shoulders and shook me. My head rattled. My vision grew dim. I heaved my legs up and kneed the thing in the groin, a useless maneuver but maybe it would distract it for a moment and I had nothing left. I was going to die. I just wanted to inflict as much damage as I could before it killed me.

Dimly, I could feel a trickle of blood leaking down the side of my face. The blood dripped onto the metal bands holding me in place. The robot froze. It held me that way for almost a minute, while I gasped for air and tried to recover my senses.

I could sense radio waves zipping back and forth between the three robots. The first one stopped its rotation. The second rose to its feet and stood still. The one holding me put me down and released its grip. I stood there, facing it, breathing deeply. It turned and walked back to the man shaped hole in the mountain and entered.

I looked at the two that were left. One of them raised a hand and waved it toward the entrance, a strangely human like gesture. I looked at the other. It stood unmoving. I took a step toward it and tried to walk around. It raised its arm, blocking my way, but otherwise made no movement.

I sighed. Apparently, I was not being given a choice, though this didn't bother me as much as it might have since it looked like I wasn't fated to be dead, at least not at the moment.

"Alright," I said. "Why not?"

I walked into the entrance and found myself in a small metal room with an airlock door on the other end. The door was open. Light flooded into the room in which I was standing. I walked through into a much larger room. The walls and the floor of this room were polished rock. Soft luminescent lights glowed from the ceiling. The room was empty of furniture.

A man stood near the far door. His arms hung at his sides and he carried no weapons. Dressed in combat fatigues and a green, military style jacket, with deep blue eyes and sandy hair, he was about my height and appeared no older than thirty. He drew a deep breath when he saw my face and he broke into a radiant smile.

"Lord Oliveros," he said. "Welcome home."

"Huh?" I said.

"Lord Damian Oliveros was Governor-General of Illyria at the time of the Hirrill invasion. This was his headquarters and principal residence."

I knew of Damian Oliveros, of course. Every school child did. His exploits were legendary. Governor General and Viceroy, Damian Oliveros had kept Illyria stable and relatively united after the Usurper, Thomas Montgomery invaded the home worlds, overthrew the crown and the Empire dissolved into ruin and civil war.

It didn't last, of course. Once Oliveros was gone, Illyria had fractured into the nation states that persist to this day. Our own civil wars and dark ages and slow ascent back to technological civilization followed, but it all would have been much worse without Damian Oliveros.

Sagittarius Command. That was the name of the ancient base. Three thousand years ago, Sagittarius Command had burrowed deep inside Mount Sindara and spread out for many kilometers down and beyond the mountain slopes. It was a city, but all traces of the city outside of the mountain were gone, eaten away by the heat and the jungle and millennia of time and multiple invasions, ground into ashes and dust. Deep underground, if an archaeologist were to dig into the jungle, he would find concrete and pottery and statues and the charred ruins of ancient buildings, now long gone. Only here, inside the mountain, was anything left.

"You, it seems, are Damian Oliveros' direct descendant. The robots are programmed to recognize certain genetic markers. Yours is one of them." He smiled ruefully. "An assumption was made that the bearers of such genetic markers would be on our side. Perhaps this assumption was naïve."

His name was Edward Lane, the Preceptor of Sagittarius Command. We sat together in a strangely mundane looking office, with a wooden desk, a couch along one wall, a couple of battered but comfortable chairs. A monitor screen, made to look like a window, displayed a scene at the base of the mountain. Winston Smith, or somebody working with him, had called in reinforcements. An army was massing there, preparing to attack.

"Our screens fell a few hours ago, not that the screens were much of an impediment. They kept out laser fire and missiles but they don't want to destroy this facility. They're trying to capture it."

I nodded. We had walked in under the screens; so had the enemy troops and their mutated apes.

"They've already taken the lower levels," Lane said with a resigned shrug. "We evacuated them years ago and all the useful tech was stripped, so we haven't lost much, yet. Still, they're wearing us down. Unless things change, we're going to be overwhelmed.

"Our ancestors had quantum teleportation. Their starships were twice as fast as current, Second Empire designs. They had machines that could read minds and transmute matter. You wanted a new house, a new chair, a larger bed? No problem, just think about it, it will arrive in the mail tomorrow. Funny, though, how much less one really desires when you can have anything at all." Lane smiled. "This was in the last days of the Empire. At first, everybody wanted a palace of their own. After a few years, most of them grew bored with showing off their stuff. After all, it was no different than anybody else's stuff. When anything material is within your grasp, just by making a wish…well, knowing you can have it is usually enough. When the pressure to make a living was removed, most people discovered that what they wanted most was to hang out with their friends." His face grew thoughtful. "And have a lot of sex," he said.

"Well, that doesn't surprise me," I said.

He shrugged. "None of this is relevant now. Unless things change, we're going to lose."

Lane's ancestors had been here for over two thousand years, watching, waiting, guiding when they could, recruiting from the outside to keep the blood lines fresh. "You can't marry your sister for two thousand years and expect good results. There weren't enough of us. In the early days, when the Empire had abandoned this planet and society everywhere was collapsing, we had hundreds of agents in the outside world, influencing events, guiding and cajoling, working for positive change. We were like the ancient Christian monasteries during the middle ages on Earth. We preserved the intellectual heritage of mankind. It was our charge, you see. Serve the Empire, serve mankind; but it's been centuries since there were enough of us to do more than maintain the status quo. During the dark ages, when technology on this planet had almost vanished, there didn't seem to be much point. Sagittarius Command was almost abandoned more than once, but there were always at least a few that tried to keep the lights on, to fulfill our mission."

"I don't understand why you couldn't do more," I said. "You were an island of stability in a world that was falling apart."

Lane frowned at me. "It's one base on one small island. It was decided very early on that our presence here had to stay secret. We were invaded more than once, you see, and the outside city was destroyed. After the first few centuries, a really determined army could have occupied us at almost any time."

I shrugged. "So, you do have these things?" I asked. "Quantum teleportation, an improved star drive, the ability to transmute matter?"

He gave me a sad smile. "No," he said, "we don't. It's possible that the plans still exist, but it's been centuries since we could access the relevant databases." He shook his head. "The Second Empire has technology beyond any on Illyria, though it is nowhere near as advanced as that of the First Empire. If they capture this facility, they may be able to access that data." He raised an eyebrow. "Or they may not. We don't know."

"Then you have a choice to make," I said.

"And what choice would that be?"

"You can choose who you give it to, or you can choose to destroy it. Perhaps you don't know it but Winston Smith has overplayed his hand. Most of the civilized world wants him dead. Say the word and I can have an armada from Meridien and our allied nations here within hours."

He shook his head. "You're not going to do that."

I frowned. "Why not? We can save you."

"Because despite whatever protestations the representatives of the Second Empire may have made, Winston Smith is not acting alone. He's an intelligence agent, and he has the full and total backing of his government. Oh, they wanted to maintain some semblance of plausible deniability but for stakes like these?" He shook his head. "If Meridien tries to get involved, they will find themselves at war with the Second Empire. Meridien cannot win such a war. No nation, no group of nations on this planet can."

I stared at him. "The Empire consul said that his government was not involved. He was telling the truth."

"You know this for a fact?"

"Yes," I said. "I can tell."

"Can you?" Lane shrugged. "Then his government was keeping him in the dark."

"Oh," I said.

"Oh, indeed. We still have our sources, you see. Even on the Eastern continent." He shrugged. "Not many, but our information is reliable."

I looked at the screen, at the army massing down below, preparing their final assault on Mount Sindara. Edward Lane looked at me looking at the enemy and then he said, "There is one possibility, one thing that might help."

My eyes snapped to his face. "Tell me more," I said.

Chapter 20

"Lord Oliveros was a crafty one. The politics of the First Empire were Byzantine, everybody plotting against everybody else, vying for power and position. He was a distant cousin of the Imperator, distant enough so that he had no realistic claim to the throne but close enough to be regarded with suspicion. It's unclear how he managed to get posted to Illyria. Maybe the Imperator's courtiers wanted him far away. Maybe this was his aim all along, because once he arrived, as viceroy, his word was absolute law.

Lane smiled. "This should do it. Ready?"

I was having serious second thoughts but I wasn't going to back out, not now. "Yeah," I said.

"Excellent." Lane puttered with the keyboard, frowning, and then the helmet descended on my head. I could feel multiple pinpoints of sharp pain, followed by numbing cold as the helmet injected local anesthetic beneath my skin. Thin delicate wires began to bore into my skull. I knew this and the thought of what was happening made me mildly nauseous, though by now, I felt no physical discomfort.

"You do know what you're doing, don't you?" I asked.

"Pretty much."

"Oh, great," I said.

"Relax. The instructions are clear."

"It's been what? Six hundred years?"

"A little longer than that—seven hundred fifty, actually, but the machines monitor themselves and undergo a full service every ten years. Don't worry; it will work."

What was it the little AI had said, back in Wittburg? Over time, errors creep into the best of programs, a stray cosmic ray, the smallest electrical charge can change the orientation of binary data. I didn't have as much confidence in this scheme, or in the sanctity of his equipment, as Edward Lane. Frankly, the whole idea was insane.

But it was the best idea we had.

Except to run, I thought. Running was an option. I was trained in hiding and good at surveillance and Lane had implied that escape tunnels under the mountain did exist. Yes...running from the fight that could no longer be avoided was most certainly an option, but not one that I wanted to take. And, of course, neither did Edward Lane.

"Lord Oliveros kept his secrets to himself. He didn't have a lot of friends and only a few trusted advisors. We know he had resources that only he could access. His second wife and youngest daughter were assassinated. He barely survived. It made him bitter and suspicious."

"No shit," I muttered.

"Hmm."

The helmet covered my eyes but my ears still functioned. I could hear Lane's fingers clattering over his keyboard.

We had sat in his cramped little office only an hour before while he explained it to me. "There were many Lords Oliveros before him but he was the best of them all, the most successful, at least. He knew how to play the game. Shortly before his death at the age of four hundred and twelve, he made a copy of his memories and personality. Only his direct descendants can access them. This has been done four times before you. A direct descendant of Lord Damian Oliveros can plug into the database and learn all of his secrets. Maybe there's something there that can save us."

"What happened to the other four?" I asked.

He looked away, frowning. "The second died during the memory transfer. The machine killed him. Apparently, he was not a direct descendent, after all. One of Lord Oliveros' daughters-in-law was rumored to have had affairs. The rumors were apparently true. The other three came through the process in good health."

"What happened to them then?"

"They all became successful. They all grew rich. None of them ever talked about what they learned."

"So, there might be nothing in these memories that can help our situation."

Edward Lane pursed his lips and frowned. "That is true."

Maybe. Maybe not. I shook my head and hoped I wouldn't regret this. "I'll do it," I said.

Lane nodded. "I thought you would."

So here I was, body strapped down to a metal chair, head enclosed in a padded metal helmet. I could feel...something. Small flashes of light appeared in front of my eyes. Distant, burbling sounds filled my ears, the sound of running water, the sound of a bird chirping…and suddenly, I was sitting in a room across from a man who looked much like me. He had a few strands of gray in his hair, sharp eyes and a suspicious mouth. He peered at my face and gave me a thin smile. "Your name?" he said.

"Douglas Oliver."

He clucked his tongue. "I am Lord Damian Oliveros. Apparently, I am your ancestor. Tell me your situation."

I did, and Lord Oliveros nodded. He reached out and touched my forehead with the tip of one finger. "Sleep," he said, and the world went dark.

In my dreams, I held the body of my daughter. Her face looked peaceful amid the wreckage of our vehicle. I looked down upon my wife. She did not look peaceful at all. Her face held a snarl, defying her killers. *Revenge*, I silently vowed. *You will both be avenged.*

It took thirty years and the loss of a son but I made good on that vow. Was it worth it? Possibly not, but at stake was more than the honor of Clan Oliveros. It was necessary for my survival and the survival of all that I had worked for to demonstrate, publicly and clearly, that violence against my family and my person would avail my enemies nothing, would instead cost them everything.

Those who wished me harm lived their lives in fear, and that was good. It was better to be feared than to be loved, because love can never be counted on and fear lasts forever.

I lived a long life, full of violence and regret but there was triumph mixed in as well. I made the world a better place. I preserved a little bit of civilization among the ruins and the ashes. All of my children, the ones who survived, fought for the Empire. Most of them never came back, but a few did, and I cherished them, as fathers have always cherished their children. I gave them everything that I could and we were strong together. We ruled this world with compassion and strength.

Here is what you seek. Here is what you need. Take it. It is yours. Use it well and wisely.

I saw another young man come before me, seeking aid. He had my face. I gave it to him. A young woman, afraid but resolute, who put on the helmet and received the knowledge that she required to defeat her enemies. Another, who sought what he had no right to, who died, and another, and now, one more.

Do not fear. It is here, and here, and here.

The Imperator stood before me while I knelt at his feet. The Imperator was wise, as always, but he was dying. We both knew this. The stars shone through the window of his ship, blazing in the endless night. "Go, Damian, before I kill you." He smiled at me. "I don't want to, but if you stay I shall probably have to. You represent too great a threat. You are too smart for my own good, and for the good of my children."

"As you command, Majesty, so shall I obey."

He smiled, a soft, knowing smile. "Of course you shall. Your loyalty has never been in question. It is the people around you who cannot be trusted."

And so I left him and I left the world of my birth and came here and prospered, as he and I both knew that I would, and you have followed after me, seeking wisdom.

Here and here and here. He/I showed me. He/I nodded, and understood.

"Do you see? Do you understand?"

"I do. I do understand."

"Good," he said, and I agreed.

Chapter 21

I groaned.

Edward Lane's face loomed over me, looking worried. "I'm alright," I said, and I was, sort of…I just wasn't sure *who* I was. The memories of Lord Damian Oliveros filled me, overlaying my own. I drew a deep breath. This was going to take a little while.

Edward Lane nodded. "Don't try to push it. It will be confusing until you incorporate the new memories." His face grew pensive. "You are now the revenant of Lord Damian Oliveros. Supposedly, in the days of the Empire, only the best and brightest were allowed to receive such memories. It was a great honor to be one of the chosen."

I shook my head, still feeling dizzy. "What happened to this Utopia that you described to me? Where anyone could have everything that he wanted?"

He gave me a smile that said I should have known better. "Any *material* thing that he wanted. The machines could never give a man respect or status or authority or power. Somebody has to give the orders. Somebody has to be in charge. These are things that men will always fight for."

Just then, a small, quick vibration came through the walls, then another. "They're breaking into the next level," Lane said. "We're losing."

"How many of you are there?" Strange that I had never asked him this, but then a lot had happened in a short period of time.

"Three hundred," he said.

Naturally. I almost laughed. "You have combat robots," I said. "How many?"

"Twenty-seven," Lane said, and I winced. Twenty-seven combat robots were worth at least five times their number in a fight, but even that was not going to be enough.

"We need to buy time," I said.

"Have you learned anything useful? Anything at all? Can you save us?"

I cocked my head to the side, considering this question. "Yes," I said, "and maybe."

"Better than nothing," he said.

Oh, yes, it was better than nothing. It was much, much better than nothing...but was it enough? "And how many men do they have?" I asked.

He hesitated. "Hard to tell. They've been taking out our sensors. Maybe two thousand."

"Where are their reinforcements coming from?" Not that it really mattered; I was just curious. It might matter in the future, I thought, if we survived this.

"We don't know. A steady stream of airships has been arriving. Finlandia is letting them through."

"Let's go," I said. "We have a lot of work to do."

Sagittarius Command, or what was left of it, consisted of seventeen levels inside Mount Sindara. The bottom two levels, the largest, had served mostly as storage and training facilities in the days of the Empire. They had been relatively easy to break into and occupy. Winston Smith and his forces had then burrowed through the rock and the inner steel lining of the next three levels. These had been living quarters, for the most part. The enemy now occupied more than fifty percent of the entire volume of Sagittarius Command. The computers, the power sources, the shield generators, the research facilities were all higher up in the mountain—for the moment, beyond their reach.

"Take me to Command Facility One A," I said.

Lane looked momentarily embarrassed. "Where is that?" he asked.

I looked at him, amazed. "You don't know?"

He shrugged.

No, I thought. Of course, he did not know. "I'll show you," I said.

Two minutes later, at the end of a seemingly blank corridor, I placed my palm upon a hidden sensor and a door slid seamlessly open. Lane's eyes grew huge. "Come," I said.

We entered a small room and three lights in the ceiling glowed. "Lord Oliveros," a soft voice said. "Where to?"

"The Eyrie," I said.

We moved upward with a smooth whoosh. Edward Lane shook his head. "We never knew this was here," he said.

"Sagittarius Command has many secrets," I said. "There's a whole separate installation that Damian Oliveros and his successors kept to themselves. Why don't you know this?"

Lane shook his head. "Six hundred years ago, there was an accident. We're not even certain what happened. The preceptor at that time was newly invested. His predecessor had recently retired and the new preceptor had not yet picked a successor. It was customary for the retiring preceptor and his replacement to go on a tour of our facilities throughout the continent. It helped to foster a smooth transfer of power and responsibility. There was a freak storm, perhaps also an explosion. It may have been sabotage. We just don't know. Their airship fell from the sky and all on board were killed." He shrugged. "Only the preceptor, and a revenant of Damien Oliveros, if one existed, possessed the codes and could access the databases. We have lost so much, over the years."

"You needed a descendent of Damien Oliveros. This place won't work without one. There must be others out there. Why didn't you look?"

He frowned at me. "The population of the city of Rome at the height of the Roman Empire was over a million, the greatest metropolis of its time. At the depths of the dark ages, only a few hundred years later, the population of Rome had fallen to barely ten thousand, ignorant and starving, scrabbling through the ruins of their ancestors. So it was with Sagittarius Command. As I've told you, this base was almost abandoned more than once. Our resources were…limited.

"Have you ever heard of the Genesis Corporation?" Lane asked.

"No," I said.

"It serves some of the same functions as your Guilds. It's a research and investment firm, and it gives financial support to new technologies. We own it. It was founded over a century ago, at the height of the industrial revolution. At that time, we still had some remnants of technology, the shield generators for instance, and fusion power, that nobody else on this world possessed. Genesis was, and remains our primary resource. Genesis has been searching for descendants of Damian Oliveros for all of its existence. It's yet to find one."

Lane shook his head. "Damien Oliveros is a distant legend. Today, his name is barely remembered but for hundreds of years, Damien Oliveros was considered the greatest hero in this world's history. Every orphan took the name of Oliveros, or Oliver, or Olivetti or some such variation. Dozens of families that could claim a plausible connection changed their names. There were hundreds. We investigated as many of them as we could. Your grandfather came from Cornwall?"

I nodded.

"The Olivers of Cornwall have no relation whatsoever to Damien Oliveros. We know this for a fact."

I frowned. "My mother, then?"

"Apparently. What was your mother's name?" Lane asked.

"Sarah Morrigan."

Lane smiled sadly. "Who would have thought? And yet here you are, the answer to our prayers, when it's too late to do us any good."

Three hundred men, and twenty-seven combat robots...I sighed to myself. The numbers didn't really matter. The plan I was considering did not depend upon mere numbers. The elevator ground to a halt. The door opened upon another blank corridor, the floor covered with a thin layer of dust. The end of the corridor opened into a small, almost blank room at the exact center of the highest level of the base, a level that appeared on no maps and was thought to be solid rock.

A small, low table circled the room. Inside the circle sat a command chair, equipped with a retractable helmet and a holoscreen. I sat in the command chair. "Sit down," I said.

Lane took a seat at the circular table, slightly behind me so that he could see the screen over my shoulder. I slid the helmet down over my head and opened my eyes. A multitude of pictures shot past on the inside of the helmet. *Stop*, I thought. *Display*, and the machine did as I ordered.

Lane sucked in his breath. Winston Smith stood on the lowest level of the installation, Derek Landry at his side. His troops were lined up at parade rest, standing on the concrete floor, rifles at their sides, hands behind their backs. Their discipline was less than I would have expected from trained troops. Some of them shifted in place. Some rolled their eyes. A few slouched and a few others looked bored. Neither Smith nor Landry seemed to mind. And why should they? They had more than enough resources to do the job.

"Winston," I said, my voice rolling like thunder in the confined space.

A stir went through the crowd. Most of them cringed. All of them raised their heads and peered wildly around. A holograph flickered against one wall and I almost laughed. It was the long dead form of Damian Oliveros, looking imperiously out over the crowd. Winston Smith cleared his throat. "Who are you?" he asked.

"I'm your worst nightmare, Winston," I said, and I almost cackled. "I'm going to kill you, Winston. I'm going to kill all of you!"

The lights in the room flickered. The hologram vanished and the crowd shifted, looking for one long moment as if they might bolt. "Silence!" Smith roared. The men started at his voice. A few stepped forward but then they shook themselves, blinked a few times, took a deep breath and slowly settled into place.

"This is just talk," Winston said, "and talk is cheap. We outnumber them ten to one. We've already taken half of this installation and we're going to take the rest. You're soldiers. Act like it."

Most of them weren't actually soldiers, I reflected. Putting a rifle in a man's hands and a uniform on his body does not automatically turn him into a soldier. They were more of a mob, but a dangerous mob, nonetheless, and they did indeed outnumber us by almost ten to one.

"Alright," I said to Edward Lane. "Here is what we're going to do."

What we were going to do was fight for every inch. We knew the territory. They didn't. If my plan worked, it would be enough to salvage at least something from this fiasco. A big *if*.

Winston Smith evidently saw no advantage in waiting. On the contrary, the longer he waited, the greater the chance we had of demoralizing his troops. His men crawled up the mountainside, occupying all the stairs and levels, and began to bore in, but it wasn't going to be easy for him. The leaders of Sagittarius Command had had many years to prepare.

At Edward Lane's order, explosive charges set into the mountain went off in sequence, from the bottom up. The mountain shook. The stairs crumbled into dust and the bodies of over one hundred soldiers evaporated into bloody mist. The stone platforms, filled with enemy troops, released from their moorings and fell into the jungle and the sea. Two hundred more of Winston Smith's men fell with them.

But that was all we had, on the outside, at least. Amid the rubble and the dust and the loose, unstable rock, five hundred more enemy troops climbed up and began to set charges of their own.

The mountain shook again.

I sat in the Eyrie with Lane, monitoring it all. At over fifty different points, enemy troops brought in miniature earth diggers and set more small charges. They had ground penetrating sensors. They knew where to seek the easiest access to the inside of the base.

Our troops waited for them. A puff of dust falling into a room: an office perhaps, a lab, even a bedroom. A hole appears, then widens and then soon after, an enemy soldier wriggles his way inside. He falls, his body riddled by bullets or cut nearly in half by hand held lasers…and so it goes, one after the other, soldier after soldier after dead and dying soldier.

For a little while, it looked like it might be enough.

The combat robots did the most damage, as we had hoped and expected, but the mutated apes were almost their match. Momentarily, the attacking soldiers fell back and let the apes take the lead and soon, at the price of over fifty dead apes, the robots were dismembered and then dismantled.

I wondered what would induce a soldier to be first into this chaos. The first one into a hail of death is going to die. No chance, no choice; but others soon follow, and the defenders are slowly, and then not so slowly, pushed back and are soon outnumbered and then the fighting rages through the halls and then, inexorably, the tide has turned. The defenders become the hunted, charging blindly down empty corridors, seeking a place to stand and attack and take back the territory that they regard as their own. Except that soon, all too soon, there is no place left to stand.

There is nothing left.

Chapter 22

Five hours had passed. Grimly, almost silently, Edward Lane and I watched the systematic destruction of Sagittarius Command, a bulwark against history that had stood for over three thousand years; and we watched with grim satisfaction as enemy troops poured into the mountain.

Winston Smith set himself up in a command center and through the thousands of small sensors set into every wall and facet of the base, we watched him watching and giving orders as his soldiers began the final mopping up. Finally, Lane turned to me. "It's over," he said. "It's time."

I nodded and threw a small switch on the command panel; the order to evacuate would be transmitted to all our remaining troops. Lane and I rose to our feet and I pressed a series of buttons set into the rocky wall. A man-sized panel slid aside. A light went on. We entered and walked down a series of stairs, turning and twisting deep beneath the surface of the mountain. It was a long walk. Half an hour later, the stairs ended in a concrete platform. At the end of the platform, beyond a metal railing and beneath a jagged, rocky ceiling, lay a seemingly endless expanse of cold, dark water that led through a series of man made caverns out into the sea.

Fifteen men waited for us on the platform, all who were left.

The night before, I had explained the situation to all three hundred inhabitants of Sagittarius Command. I told them what the memories of Lord Damian Oliveros had revealed to me. I explained the plan that Edward Lane and I had devised and I asked for volunteers. I asked for fifty to remain. I knew none of them, of course, but they all knew me, or at least, they knew what the ghost of Damian Oliveros meant to them and to their hopes for the future. Almost all of the three hundred had volunteered and Edward Lane selected the ones he wanted. All the rest of the men and women of Sagittarius Command left shortly after.

And of the fifty who had stayed to fight, only these fifteen remained.

"Thank you," I said. "Thank you all."

They were bloody, aching and tired. Most bore injuries, but they were unbowed. One of them, a large, bearded man with unruly black hair and sharp blue eyes, looked for a moment like he was about to say something, then he gave a tired grimace and merely shrugged.

Damian Oliveros had been a brilliant man. I doubt that he foresaw this exact scenario, but close enough. I walked over to the sheer rock wall and pulled open a panel. Behind the panel sat a metal box, and inside the box were five colored plastic buttons. I pushed them in the proper sequence and a holographic display lit up all around me. Suddenly, I was sitting behind a desk in an office, except that it was not my face that appeared in the holo. It was the face of Damian Oliveros, with a framed painting of Mount Sindara on the wall behind me and a vase full of cut flowers standing on the desk by my side. Sagittarius Command was riddled with such installations, all unobtrusive, all hidden, most in plain sight. Damian Oliveros and his successors had wanted to be able to function in their appointed role as Governor-General from anywhere in the base and at any time.

"Attention," I said, and my voice echoed out along the platform that we stood on and out into all the rooms and hallways and into every corner of Sagittarius Command, and on every screen in the facility, the face of Damian Oliveros smiled down upon them. "This is Lord Damian Oliveros speaking. My message to you is simple. Observe." I held up a small handheld and compressed the top. Somewhere, high above our heads, the mountain shuddered. Even here, thousands of meters below, we could feel the vibration. A gout of flame spewed out into the sky and rocks and boulders rained down upon the jungle and the sea.

I gave them a moment to digest what had just happened and then I spoke again. "What you have just observed was merely a demonstration, so that all of you will clearly understand me and believe what I am about to say. There are almost two thousand enemy troops inside Sagittarius Command at this moment, a rag tag band of thieves and murderers pretending to be an army, and it is this band of thieves and murderers that I am now addressing. The forces that have attempted to resist your invasion have been defeated and are now nearly destroyed. You sought to capture this base and in this, you have succeeded, but now this base has captured you. As I have just demonstrated, the Sagittarius Command has been mined with explosives.

"It is my judgment that there is no possible accommodation by which this situation can be resolved. Even if you put down your arms and leave here now, a perpetual siege of Sindara and a continued assault on Sagittarius Command seems inevitable. Such a situation is not acceptable. So,"—I gave a thin, bright eyed smile into the camera—"in one hour and fifteen minutes from this moment, Sagittarius Command shall cease to exist. Any living thing within three kilometers of this installation shall cease to exist as well. You have been warned."

I reached forward and pushed the button. My face vanished from the screens. "Let's get out of here," I said.

Winston Smith rose from his seat, his face white, his hands trembling in rage. His staff ignored him as they piled out of their makeshift command center. He was tempted for a moment to order them to stop but then, what was the point? They would merely disobey him and what was he going to tell them to do, anyway? No. He slowly shook his head. This was a fiasco, but he was a professional. Some ventures succeed. Some fail. A professional knows when it becomes necessary to cut one's losses.

Time to leave, but as he walked toward the door, it slid closed. Four men besides himself were left in the room. He stared at them then grasped the handle on the door and tried to turn it. Nothing happened. He stepped back. "Open it," he said.

One of the men stepped forward and grasped the handle. "It won't turn."

A voice filled the room—my voice. "The amnesty that you have been offered does not apply to Winston Smith," I said. "All the rest of you can leave. Not him."

The men looked at each other, then one of them gave a sheepish grin and said, "Well, Winston, it's been nice knowing you."

A gun suddenly appeared in Winston Smith's hand. "You're not leaving without me. Open that door."

"The door will not open so long as you are holding a gun," I said.

A shot rang out then another, and Winston Smith's body slumped to the ground. The two men holstered their weapons, shrugged and turned toward the door. "Sorry about that, Winston," one of them muttered.

All-in-all, I thought, I liked the way that went.

The door opened. The men exited and the door closed. Winston Smith drew one final breath and lay still.

I was tempted to deal with Derek Landry the same way but in the end, Derek Landry was only a mercenary. He wasn't in charge and I felt confident that after this debacle, he would return to his well-deserved obscurity. I let him go with all the rest.

And so the forces of the People's Army had been warned and my conscience was now clear, which I almost regretted, just a little. I had seriously considered blowing the place up with all of them inside but this seemed...excessive. I shrugged to myself. They had an hour left to get out of Sagittarius Command and they were on their own.

Fuck 'em.

I shut down the hologram, vanished from the screens and left the rampaging soldiers of the People's Army to their own devices. When I turned around and faced Edward Lane and his fifteen surviving men, I found them staring dubiously at the mechanism of our hoped for deliverance. Three of them, actually. Three submarines moored by the railing, capable of carrying perhaps twenty men each, vessels that had floated here in these dark, cold waters for over two thousand years, waiting for just this moment.

I shared their concern but I needn't have worried. Damian Oliveros and his successors had known what they were doing. The automatic maintenance still functioned. The subs were clean and shiny and looked almost new. We took all three of them. Edward Lane and five others entered the first sub together with me. The controls barely existed. A voice asked, "Identify yourselves."

"I am Douglas Oliver," I said, "the revenant of Lord Damian Oliveros."

One by one, all the men stated their names and their reasons for being here. Once the last one spoke, the voice was silent for a few moments then said, "You are all approved transport. Where do you wish to go?"

"First, take us out to sea," I said. "We need to be more than three kilometers from this base within,"—I glanced at my interface—"forty-five minutes."

The voice said nothing. The engines started with a smooth hum. We descended beneath the surface, water swiftly rising to cover the portholes. All functions operated smoothly and we moved forward. Thirty-seven minutes later, we rose to the surface. A hatch opened, and we clambered out onto the deck.

It was dusk. The sun was beginning to set, a purple and orange ball just touching the horizon. Two of the first, brightest stars were already visible overhead and both moons glowed in the sky. There was no wind and the waters around our vessel were calm. Mount Sindara rose behind us, jagged and defiant. No hint of the recent destruction could be seen. I glanced again at my interface. "Six seconds," I said.

The mountain shuddered. Small puffs of smoke rose from the base, then more of them, ascending steadily toward the summit. The sharp sound of distant explosions and boulders cracking and crashing down into the jungle came to our ears. Mount Sindara seemed to slump inward upon itself. A portion of the summit came loose and slid down, picking up speed as it went and plummeted into the surrounding sea. And then there was silence.

The men around me sighed. Some shook their heads. A few wiped their eyes. Sagittarius Command had been their home, for most of them, the only home they had ever known.

"And so, it ends," Edward Lane whispered.

"One chapter ends; another chapter begins," I said. "It's a brave new world out there. You'll find a place."

He gave me a tired grin. "I suppose."

"You will." I smiled. "And besides, I'm rich. I can always use a few good men."

Chapter 23

I activated the transponder and an hour later, we rendezvoused with the Meridien sub that had dropped me on the island. The other four men that had gone in with Curtis and I had left the Sindara yesterday. One team had scouted the coastline, the other had gathered intel on the Gath and Finlandia assets moored in the harbor. All four had escaped detection and successfully completed their missions.

I gave the captain a brief report on my activities and decided to remain with the men and ships of Sagittarius Command. Three days later, all four subs entered the sheltered harbor of Meridien. The water was green and clear. A gentle breeze stirred a scatter of foam on top of the waves. The sky was very blue. Pennants fluttered in the wind. Crowds waved, not at us exactly, but at all the ships in the harbor, and the ships' crews waved back. It was a welcome, familiar sight and I felt my spirits lift. "Home," I said.

Edward Lane stared all around, wide eyed. "It's crowded."

It was, wasn't it? The greatest city in the world. "You'll get used to it."

Lane gave a half-hearted grin. "I suppose I will," he said doubtfully.

"Before we leave, there's one more thing I wanted to ask you," I said.

Edward Lane looked at me, standing there on the deck in the sunlight.

"Why did you allow me to purchase the rights to Sindara? I assume that the family that owned them belonged to you?"

"Of course," he said. "They did as we instructed."

"So, why?"

Edward Lane sighed. "Do you know how the population of this world has grown, in the past hundred years?"

"A lot. I don't know the exact amount."

"The dark ages are long since over. We've had our Renaissance and our Enlightenment and our industrial revolution, and then the Second Empire came and things changed even more. Infant mortality has been largely abolished. Health care is almost universal. Nobody starves. The population is ten times larger than it was a hundred years ago and very few of them need to worry about basic survival, not anymore. People are concerned with status and money and having a good time."

"So?" I asked.

"Sindara is a tropical island with beautiful beaches and a pleasant climate that varies little with the seasons. Sooner or later, somebody was going to want to develop its resources. We realized that if we tried to keep it fallow, it would become apparent that somebody was manipulating the situation, that something was not right. We decided to pre-empt that eventuality. You would have developed the Southern portion of the island. A few years later, we would have developed, or allowed to be developed, the rest. People would live there. Towns and even cities would grow. Nobody would have found this suspicious, and Sagittarius Command could have continued as before, hiding in plain sight."

"So, I was meant to be a front," I said.

"Of course. You were convenient." He smiled. "Your name amused us. It seemed somehow appropriate. We didn't realize how appropriate it really was, and we didn't count on Gath, or Finlandia or the Second Empire."

I looked around at the harbor and the people waving and smelled the clean, fresh air, and I shook my head sadly. "It was a good plan," I said. "It's too bad it didn't work out."

He shrugged. "Sometimes they don't."

I gave my report to the council, an edited version, since there were a few facts that I felt it wiser to keep to myself. I saw both Leon Sebastian and Guild Master Anderson looking at me with narrowed eyes, but neither said anything at all while I spoke. The rest of the council hung on my words and when I finished, Ballister said, "The submarines that you returned with are more advanced than any known design. Their avionics and controls are far beyond our current technology. It's a pity that all the rest was destroyed."

After the destruction of Sagittarius Command, the three Gath destroyers had steamed away. They were now moored in the harbor of Finlandia's nearest naval base. The government of Gath was negotiating for their return. The Finlandia patrol ships still remained around the island, some of them at least, but the advance base that the Second Empire had established on the opposite coast from Sagittarius Command was deserted.

Most of the soldiers who invaded the base had gotten out in time. Perhaps a hundred, those who were highest in the mountain and who had the furthest to go, were still too close and perished when the mountain exploded.

I shrugged. "Better to destroy it than let it fall into enemy hands and if it still existed, it would always be an incitement to open conflict. None of us need that."

"But you knew that you couldn't win," Ballister said. "You didn't have the resources. Why did you bother to fight? Why didn't you simply evacuate the base and then destroy it. You lost thirty-five men, for nothing."

I sighed. "Not for nothing. Believe me, I considered that option, but if we had done as you suggest, the Second Empire would have assumed—correctly—that the men and women of Sagittarius Command had escaped. They would have also assumed—incorrectly—that they had taken the data that the Empire wanted with them. No. We needed to make a stand. We needed to have the Empire believe, without any question, that we were fighting to the bitter end to protect whatever secrets were in that base." I shrugged. "They would never have stopped searching. None of the survivors would have ever been safe."

Ballister frowned and sank back into his seat. "I suppose so." He did not sound entirely convinced. I didn't blame him. Neither was I. I had made the best decision that I could make under the circumstances but I would always wonder.

After another hour of aimless questioning, they dismissed me.

I spent the rest of the afternoon going over the current state of my business with Benedict and the rest of my administrative team. As before, I had to force myself to pay attention. The minutiae of cash flow, accounts receivable and opportunities for profit maximization seemed somehow entirely irrelevant to my current existence, though I knew, intellectually, that they were not. The threat analysis, that listing of actual and potential attacks on either my business or my person, seemed particularly juvenile after my recent adventures. Finally, I sighed. "Okay, Gentlemen, I understand. Thank you very much. We'll pick it up tomorrow, first thing."

I saw Benedict give a worried glower to Josh Cantor, his aide, a thin, well dressed young guy, newly out of collegium and eager to prove his worth. Something about this interaction amused me, but I couldn't say exactly what.

I glanced at the clock on the wall. Two hours. In two more hours, I would see Jennifer. I wondered how it would go. Perhaps not quite the way she expected. I looked at the clock again and frowned.

Two hours later, I walked into Arcadia. She was already seated and she gave me a sly smile as I walked over and sat down. I returned the smile and just sat there for a few moments, breathing, feeling the sense of home, the serenity of being just exactly where I wanted to be, and with whom I wanted to be, wash over me.

She didn't say anything, just smiled and then looked down at her menu, frowning in concentration.

A minute later, Selene Reynolds walked up to us. "Nice to see you again," she said.

Jennifer examined her then glanced at me, suddenly no longer smiling, which made me smile more.

"Can I take your drinks order?" Selene was a very smart girl. She knew when to ignore the obvious.

"A bottle of wine," I said. "This one—from Wittburg." I pointed it out.

"Anything else? Ma'am?"

"No, thank you," Jennifer said. "Just water."

"Coming right up." Selene smiled and walked over to the next table. Jennifer followed her with her eyes.

"That Selene, pretty girl, isn't she?" I said.

Jennifer's gaze snapped to my face. She narrowed her eyes. "Don't push your luck," she said.

"Wouldn't dream of it."

By the time our wine arrived, Jennifer had recovered her good mood. We started the meal with seafood bisque, then shared a duck with blackberry sauce and wild rice. By the time dessert arrived, we were both feeling sleepy. They had allowed the room to darken as the sun set outside and candles glowed on every table. Very elegant, I thought. Nurturing.

"So, Jennifer," I said. "When did you decide to kill Graham Reid?"

She sputtered on the water she was drinking, coughed a few times and wiped her lips with a napkin. She blinked at me. "What did you say?"

I gave her a sleepy, satisfied smile. "It was obvious when I thought about it. His throat was slit. He had a knife wound in his side and another on his right arm. You like knives. You're good with them."

She frowned, clucked her tongue against her teeth. "The fact that I like knives is evidence of exactly nothing."

"Not by itself, but when you were a junior in collegium, you spent a year at Stabler University: junior year abroad, enlarge your horizons by spending time in a foreign culture. Your record was excellent, by the way." I lifted my glass of wine in salute then took a long sip. "Great wine," I said. "How do you like it?"

"It's not bad." She frowned.

"Right. Where was I? Oh, yes…Stabler, it turns out, is a small school with a very large endowment. Most of their students are there on full scholarship."

She looked at me warily, saying nothing.

"Shall I go on?"

She gave a tiny frown and sipped her wine.

"I wondered about it. Stabler's funding comes from the Genesis Corporation. The Genesis Corporation, it turns out, was fully owned by Sagittarius Command. Since Sagittarius Command no longer exists, Genesis' future is…uncertain, I guess you could say." I frowned again. "I'm not sure what that means for Stabler, but then I don't really care, now do I?

"I just couldn't help wondering, though. When I was in Sindara, I had a few moments to access their databases. You've been on their payroll all along. Did you even know that?"

"No," she said. She gave me a long look and wrinkled her brow then laughed softly. "No, so far as I knew, I was working for Genesis." She was telling the truth and I felt something deep inside of me unclench at the realization. Jennifer sat back in her seat and grimaced at her glass of wine. "My family didn't have a lot of money. Genesis paid my way through school and gave me a job. It wasn't much of a job and it didn't take much of my time: report on events in Aphelion. What exactly is wrong with that?"

"Nothing," I said, and I smiled. "Nothing at all." Then I asked, "Was I a part of your mission?"

She reared back, offended. "No, you jackass," she said.

She was telling the truth. I nodded, let out the breath I didn't realize I was holding, ate a bite of my duck and sipped my wine. It really was very good wine.

"They had a special class for us at Stabler. I wasn't the only one. They taught us what to look for, what they were interested in: shifts in the political environment, new developments, things that might result in change. Genesis is an investment advisory firm, or at least that was their cover. They do quantitative analysis on social and political trends. Their reports to select clients are highly regarded and they charge quite a lot for their services. I think Genesis will do just fine on its own." She shrugged. "I made friends with some of the other girls. We were from all over and after we graduated, most of us returned home. I stay in touch with a lot of them. We all have high IQ's. We could see what was happening. The pattern was pretty clear."

I winced at that. I thought I was good at spotting patterns and I hadn't seen a thing. Then again, my perspective had been smaller. I didn't have a network of smart young associates spread out over the continent, trained to observe and report on social trends, technological advancements and political unrest. I considered. That would have to change.

It occurred to me that Genesis might appreciate a new co-investor.

"Graham Reid was out of control," Jennifer said. "I had him followed. He wanted you dead. At the time, Winston Smith was attempting a military takeover of Meridien. He had bigger concerns than Graham Reid. He told Reid to do whatever he wanted." Jennifer gave me a thin smile. "I wasn't going to allow that."

"Did you do it yourself?"

She gave me a level look. "Daryl and Claudia were with me. They helped." She grinned faintly. "Do you think I'm stupid?"

"Not at all."

"Damn right," she said.

I nodded. The lights were low, the candles flickering. The diners were well dressed. It looked so peaceful, so civilized. I smiled. "Let's get out of here," I said.

She smiled. "Okay," she said. "Let's."

Chapter 24

Guild Master Anderson retired soon after to his estate on the mainland. I found myself a not so reluctant celebrity and I used that status for all it was worth. I was well known and at least moderately popular and Leon Sebastian pulled whatever strings he could reach. I was elected to be the next Guild Master and assumed Argent's place on the Council. Somewhere deep inside me, Lord Damian Oliveros was pleased.

Jennifer and I married. We had three children over the next ten years and then decided to wait awhile before having any more. We had time. After all, a humble little clam that lives an unobtrusive life off the coast of Iceland possesses a lifespan that exceeds five hundred years and the simple glass sponge can live for over 20,000. There is something called the Hayflick limit, which states that cells can divide no more than fifty times before they die. A structure exists on each chromosome called a telomere, and with each cellular division a small portion of the telomere is lost. After fifty or so divisions, there is no more telomere; but an enzyme called telomerase can prevent telomeres from shortening and prevent the cell from dying. Lord Damian Oliveros possessed the genes for high levels of telomerase, and so do I. Jennifer, it turns out, does not, but that is of little concern since one of the first things that the Second Empire offered us in trade, after their re-discovery of this world, was effective life extension. Very few human beings, here or throughout the human settled worlds, those that the Second Empire has reached, at least, live fewer than three hundred years. We have plenty of time.

My brother Jimmy never joined a Guild and was content to run his pub. He opened a second across the city and then a third and within a few years found himself the owner of a thriving restaurant chain. He grumbled about it now and then. "I didn't want to be a wage slave. I didn't want to owe money. I wanted to work for myself. Now, I'm owned by the business." He always said it as if he could not quite figure out how it all happened but he sounded more bemused than bothered. He liked the fact that he had succeeded on his own terms. Jennifer and I spent many happy evenings at one or another of his establishments.

Jennifer and Jolene Sebastian were already friends and though I never again felt that I could trust him completely, so were Leon and I. Our growing families spent a lot of time together. Leon and I often discussed how we might take over the world. I'm not sure if we were serious.

Edward Lane had many talents. He had run an enormous enterprise for a very long time. He knew how to prioritize and he knew how to keep his eye on the bottom line. I offered him a position as my Chief of Staff. He refused, however. A few months after the destruction of Mount Sindara, he left Meridien. "I'm going East," he said to me. "I want to see what the Empire is doing. I might go offworld."

I wished him luck and didn't see him again for many years.

A few months after my return home, Jennifer and I travelled to Gath for the wedding of Celim Bakar and Janelle Madarik. We met his brother, who was almost as big as Celim and looked much like him. Nasim Bakar was now Prime Minister of Gath. Celim had the title of Foreign Minister; he was chosen for that position at least partly because of his relationship with me. Celim and Janelle had fourteen children over the next twenty years, so I guess he did take advantage of his unlimited breeding rights. We remain good friends and they visit us often.

Meridien prospered, as did Gath. Nasim Bakar opened his nation up to the outside world. He liberalized the economy and encouraged the growth of both private industry and a middle class. After he retired, his brother Celim took over and continued his reforms.

Finlandia sponsored an expedition into the ruins of Mount Sindara but the explosives had done what they were supposed to do. There was truly nothing left. A year or so later, I took one of the submarines back to the island and explored the underground escape tunnel. It ended abruptly in a fall of rock. Still, Finlandia was taking no chances. They bored into the rubble, placed tons more explosives and reduced the mountain down to sea level. A pleasant tropical lagoon now sits where Mount Sindara once rose from the sea.

The government of Finlandia, ostracized for its support of Gath and the Second Empire's ambitions, soon fell. The new administration lost interest and I considered it poetic justice to purchase the island of Sindara once again. The first luxury resort, the first upscale beachside apartments and the largest casino in the Western hemisphere were soon welcoming tourists and my partners and I made a lot of money.

The Second Empire denied everything and maintains to this day that Miles Drayton and his colleagues were operating on their own. Nobody believes them, but they've behaved ever since. And who knows? Drayton had backers, somewhere in their government, but governments are large and have many factions. It is possible that these backers did indeed represent a rogue faction, or at least a minority opinion. We don't know, and we don't really care, just so long as they leave us alone.

On a whim, I did buy a vineyard in Wittburg and constructed a chateau in the mountains overlooking Lake April. I made a sizable donation to the Museum of History and Antiquities, in return for which they ceded me ownership of the ancient, First Empire game console. I've established it in the chateau's family room and given the little AI free run of the web, for which he is profoundly grateful. Jennifer and I travel there with the children at least once a year. They love the place and the wines really are very good.

I waited. I've been biding my time. I know that the Second Empire is still out there, not quite as benign and well meaning as they would have us all believe. I can see the patterns. I know what they've been doing. They kept an eye on me for over ten years but then there was some crisis in some far-flung region of space, something to do with an alien race and an attempted invasion of an Empire world and they seemed to lose interest in the very minor planet of Illyria.

An improved star drive, quantum teleportation, machines that can read minds and transmute matter. These marvels and many others were all lost when the First Empire fell.

But Damian Oliveros knew where to find them.

Listed on no map of First Empire cities or installations, there is a place, a very secret place, high in the desert in the middle of the continent. Nobody ever goes there, but hidden in a small, parched valley beneath a pile of rocks is a metal door, and behind the door lies a small, air cooled installation.

Deep in the jungles of the Southern Continent, hidden on an overgrown plateau there is another, and on Charon, the nearest moon, there is a third that contains the entrance to a pocket universe seeded with alien life, a universe where time flows a hundred thousand times faster than it does here. Who knows what that life has evolved into?

All still functioning, all still waiting to be discovered; and I wait as well, waiting and wondering, watching my children grow and my personal empire expand, biding my time, playing the game.

—The End—

Information about the Chronicles of the Second Interstellar Empire of Mankind

I hope you enjoyed *The City of Ashes*.

The series continues with *The Empire of Dust*, in which Michael Glover, a soldier of the First Interstellar Empire of Mankind is unexpectedly awakened after two thousand years in stasis and finds himself at the center of a plot to subvert the Second Interstellar Empire. Please read on for a preview of *The Empire of Dust: Book Three of the Chronicles of the Second Interstellar Empire of Mankind.*

For more information, please visit my website, http://www.robertikatz.com or my Facebook page, https://www.facebook.com/Robertikatzofficial/. For continuing updates regarding new releases, author appearances and general information about my books and stories, sign up for my newsletter/email list at http://www.robertikatz.com/join and you will also receive two **free short stories.** The first is a science fiction story, entitled "Adam," about a scientist who uses a tailored retrovirus to implant the Fox P2 gene (sometimes called the language gene) into a cage full of rats and a mouse named Adam, and the unexpected consequences that result. The second is a prequel to the Kurtz and Barent mysteries, entitled "Something in the Blood," featuring Richard Kurtz as a young surgical resident on an elective rotation in the Arkansas mountains, solving a medical mystery that spans two tragic generations.

Preview: The Empire of Dust: Book Three of the Chronicles of the Second Interstellar Empire of Mankind

Prologue

He groaned as the cold slowly seeped into his awareness. Dimly, he felt that he might have shivered but he wasn't certain of this. He was numb. Am I alive? He thought that he must be. I think, therefore...how did that go? Something. The thought hung there in the back of his brain, elusive. Slowly, he wriggled his fingers, then his toes. He tried to blink his eyes but the darkness was absolute. Maybe he succeeded. He couldn't tell. Fingers and toes then. He wriggled them again then clenched his fists. *If I have hands then I must have arms, and legs.* That was a comforting thought. Arms and legs were good, at least a start. He tried to cry out but something liquid and harsh filled his mouth.

Wait, a voice seemed to say. Everything will be explained. Give it time. Was this his own thought or did it come from somewhere outside? Something that might have been amusement filled his mind. He had nowhere to go and nothing but time.

For a time then, he slept.

Chapter 1

The planet was dusty, almost barren, but there was life. It clustered around the oases and on the coast. People struggling to make a living. Their database listed the world as Baldur-3, the third world in the Baldur system. The local web was unshielded and easy to access. The city below them was called Norwich.

"What do you think?" Michael Glover asked.

"We need fuel," Romulus said. "They have fuel."

Deuterium for the fusion generators. They had jumped far and this was the first human settled world they had come across in over a month that was more than a series of ruins. "I don't know," Glover said. "They're not high tech."

"High enough. The world is clean and orderly. There are three universities on the Western continent and another five on the Eastern. They're not barbarians. They'll have what we need."

Glover shrugged. "Better than nothing."

The ship's sensors had revealed a landing field on a large island off the coast of the Eastern continent. He instructed the AI to approach. They were hailed when still fifty kilometers up. "Unknown ship. State your business and world of origin."

"This is the starship London," Michael said. "Out of Beta Ionis-4." It was nonsense, of course. Beta Ionis was a rocky, frozen system with a population of sentient, low temperature aliens that had never developed interstellar travel. Humanity had been trading with them for thousands of years.

The voice seemed to hesitate. "We have no record of human habitation in the Beta Ionis system."

"We maintain a habitat in the asteroid belt." This was true, or it was true in the days of the Empire. Regardless, it was not a statement that could be disproven from half a galaxy away.

"Please state your business."

"I wish to purchase deuterium."

"The names of your crew?"

"There is only myself. My name is Michael Glover."

After a moment, the voice said. "You may land. Please follow the beacon to slip number eight."

Twenty minutes later, the London settled into the designated location. Up close, the port was busier than Michael had expected. Cargo carriers rolled across the dusty tarmac. Three other slips were occupied, all with ships somewhat smaller than their own. "I think you should stay aboard," Michael said. "Actually, you should stay hidden."

Romulus looked nothing like *Homo Sapiens*. His matte black composite structure possessed arms, legs and a head only as a concession to human sensibilities. Romulus nodded. Without a word, he pressed a panel in the wall of the main cabin. The panel slid open. The robot entered and the panel slid seamlessly closed.

Five minutes later, the port inspectors, one small, young and female, the other male, of indeterminate age, with a harried expression arrived. Michael pressed a button. A metal ramp unfolded and the main airlock opened. The inspectors entered, glancing curiously around the cabin. "Captain Glover?" The male inspector held out a hand. Michael took it. "I'm Chief Inspector Mark Conway. This is Assistant Inspector Natalie Levin. Welcome to Baldur."

Natalie Levin frowned. "You're really the only one aboard? I've heard of fully automated ships. I've never seen one."

Michael smiled. "We're proud of it. It's a copy of an ancient First Empire design."

"Well, we'll need to inspect your cargo."

"Feel free."

The cargo had been carefully chosen. Little of it was high tech, mainly inexpensive but long since out-of-date pre-fab matrices and solid state transistors that could be adapted to a variety of computer platforms, spices from five different worlds that had been stored in liquid nitrogen for over two thousand years, a lockbox of uncut jewels, most of them unique to their own worlds of origin, another lockbox containing small ingots of gold and another of platinum, and palettes of spider silk from the jungles of Rigel.

Natalie Levin pursed her lips when she saw the manifest and frowned at Michael. "You can't trade the spices here unless you get authorization from the medical authorities declaring them safe for human consumption. Also, the matrices might contain viruses that our own computers aren't equipped to handle. You're not allowed to sell them or let them connect to the local web. The rest of it is approved." She tore a sheet of paper off a clipboard. "Post this in your cargo bay where prospective buyers can see it. Good luck."

"An interesting cargo," Conway said. "You've travelled widely."

"It's what I do," Michael said. "Buy low and sell high." It was a plausible statement but not exactly the truth. It could easily become the truth, however. He had to do something to occupy his time and whatever that ultimately turned out to be, an itinerant merchant captain made an excellent cover.

"Your papers are in order," Conway said. "I suggest that you head over to the merchant's guild. They'll put you in touch with potential buyers." He glanced at a comp on his wrist. "Too late tonight, though. They open first thing in the morning."

"Thank you," Michael said. "I'll do that. Meanwhile, what is there to do at night in your fair city?" Calling it a city was definitely a stretch but it never hurt to be polite.

Natalie snorted. "Not much," she said.

Conway smiled at her. "We have some excellent restaurants, a zoo and a museum. There are a number of local sports teams but none of them are playing this evening. Two small theaters offer live entertainment. One of them is playing *Twelfth Night*, the 5714 translation. Also, the local web carries numerous channels. If you want to get off your ship, there are three reasonable hotels in the center of town." He shrugged. "Good luck."

They shook hands again, Michael thanked them both and waited until they had gone and the airlock closed behind them before saying, "What do you think?"

Romulus' voice issued from a speaker grid near the ceiling. "Everything seems in order. I'm not expecting trouble."

"No," Michael said. "It all seems very civilized."

Printed in Great Britain
by Amazon

31246949R00088